Untouched by Hu

Robert Sheckley (1928–2005) was born in New York City and raised in New Jersey. He joined the army and served in Korea in 1946–8, where, he said, he worked as '38th parallel guard, assistant newspaper editor, contracts and payroll clerk and, finally, guitarist in an army dance band'. On returning home to New York, he gained a degree and took a job in an aircraft factory, which he gave up on selling his first story to a magazine. His work appeared regularly in science-fiction magazines such as *Galaxy*, *Fantastic* and *Astounding Science Fiction* throughout the 1950s and 1960s. In 1965, the story 'Seventh Victim', from his debut collection *Untouched by Human Hands*, was made into the cult classic film *The 10th Victim*, starring Marcello Mastroianni and Ursula Andress. In total, Sheckley wrote more than four hundred short stories and fifteen novels, including the classic *Dimension of Miracles* (1968). In 2001, he was made Author Emeritus by the Science Fiction and Fantasy Writers of America.

PENGUIN CLASSICS SCIENCE FICTION

Untouched
by
Human Hands

ROBERT SHECKLEY

PENGUIN BOOKS

PENGUIN CLASSICS

UK | USA | Canada | Ireland | Australia
India | New Zealand | South Africa

Penguin Classics is part of the Penguin Random House
group of companies whose addresses can be found at
global.penguinrandomhouse.com.

First published by Ballantine Books in the United States
of America 1954
Published with this contents by Michael Joseph in
Great Britain 1955
First published in Penguin Classics Science Fiction 2021
001

Set in 11/13 pt Dante MT Std
Typeset by Integra Software Services Pvt. Ltd, Pondicherry
Printed in Great Britain by Clays Ltd, Elcograf S.p.A.

The authorized representative in the EEA is Penguin Random
House Ireland, Morrison Chambers, 32 Nassau Street,
Dublin D02 YH68

A CIP catalogue record for this book is available
from the British Library

ISBN: 978-0-241-47302-3

www.greenpenguin.co.uk

To Barbara

Contents

The Monsters

Cordovir and Hum stood on the rocky mountain-top, watching the new thing happen. Both felt rather good about it. It was undoubtedly the newest thing that had happened for some time.

'By the way the sunlight glints from it,' Hum said, 'I'd say it is made of metal.'

'I'll accept that,' Cordovir said, 'but what holds it up in the air?'

They both stared intently down to the valley where the new thing was happening. A pointed object was hovering over the ground. From one end of it poured a substance resembling fire.

'It's balancing on the fire,' Hum said. 'That should be apparent even to your old eyes.'

Cordovir lifted himself higher on his thick tail, to get a better look. The object settled to the ground and the fire stopped.

'Shall we go down and have a closer look?' Hum asked.

'All right. I think we have time – wait! What day is this?'

Hum calculated silently, then said, 'The fifth day of Luggat.'

'Damn!' Cordovir said. 'I have to go home and kill my wife.'

'It's a few hours before sunset,' Hum said. 'I think you have time to do both.'

Cordovir wasn't sure. 'I'd hate to be late.'

'Well, then, you know how fast I am,' Hum said. 'If it gets late, I'll hurry back and kill her myself. How about that?'

'That's very decent of you.' Cordovir thanked the younger man and together they slithered down the steep mountain-side.

In front of the metal object both men halted and stood up on their tails.

'Rather bigger than I thought,' Cordovir said, measuring the metal object with his eye. He estimated that it was slightly longer than their village, and almost half as wide. They crawled a circle around it, observing that the metal was tooled, presumably by human tentacles.

In the distance the smaller sun had set.

'I think we had better get back,' Cordovir said, noting the cessation of light.

'*I* still have plenty of time.' Hum flexed his muscles complacently.

'Yes, but a man likes to kill his own wife.'

'As you wish.' They started off to the village at a brisk pace.

In his house, Cordovir's wife was finishing supper. She had her back to the door, as etiquette required. Cordovir killed her with a single flying slash of his tail, dragged her body outside, and sat down to eat.

After meal and meditation he went to the Gathering. Hum, with the impatience of youth, was already there, telling of the metal object. He probably bolted his supper, Cordovir thought with mild distaste.

After the youngster had finished, Cordovir gave his own observations. The only thing he added to Hum's account was an idea: that the metal object might contain intelligent beings.

'What makes you think so?' Mishill, another elder, asked.

'The fact that there was fire from the object as it came down,' Cordovir said, 'joined to the fact that the fire stopped after the object was on the ground. Some being, I contend, was responsible for turning it off.'

'Not necessarily,' Mishill said. The village men talked about it late into the night. Then they broke up the meeting, buried the various murdered wives, and went to their homes.

Lying in the darkness, Cordovir discovered that he hadn't made up his mind as yet about the new thing. Presuming it contained intelligent beings, would they be moral? Would they have a sense of right and wrong? Cordovir doubted it, and went to sleep.

The next morning every male in the village went to the metal object. This was proper, since the functions of males were to examine new things and to limit the female population. They formed a circle around it, speculating on what might be inside.

'I believe they will be human beings,' Hum's elder brother Esktel said. Cordovir shook his entire body in disagreement.

'Monsters, more likely,' he said. 'If you take into account—'

'Not necessarily,' Esktel said. 'Consider the logic of our physical development! A single focusing eye—'

'But in the great Outside,' Cordovir said, 'there may be many strange races, most of them non-human. In the infinitude—'

'Still,' Esktel put in, 'the logic of our—'

'As I was saying,' Cordovir went on, 'the chance is infinitesimal that they would resemble us. Their vehicle, for example. Would we build—'

'But on strictly logical grounds,' Esktel said, 'you can see—'

That was the third time Cordovir had been interrupted. With a single movement of his tail he smashed Esktel against the metal object. Esktel fell to the ground, dead.

'I have often considered my brother a boor,' Hum said. 'What were you saying?'

But Cordovir was interrupted again. A piece of metal set in the greater piece of metal squeaked, turned and lifted, and a creature came out.

Cordovir saw at once that he had been right. The thing that crawled out of the hole was twin-tailed. It was covered to its top with something partially metal and partially hide. And its colour! Cordovir shuddered.

The thing was the colour of wet, flayed flesh.

All the villagers had backed away, waiting to see what the thing would do. At first it didn't do anything. It stood on the metal surface, and a bulbous object that topped its body moved from side to side. But there were no accompanying body movements to give the gesture meaning. Finally, the thing raised both tentacles and made noises.

'Do you think it's trying to communicate?' Mishill asked softly.

Three more creatures appeared in the metal hole, carrying metal sticks in their tentacles. The things made noises at each other.

'They are decidedly not human,' Cordovir said firmly. 'The next question is, are they moral beings?' One of the things crawled down the metal side and stood on the ground. The rest pointed their metal sticks at the ground. It seemed to be some sort of religious ceremony.

'Could anything so hideous be moral?' Cordovir asked, his hide twitching with distaste. Upon closer inspection, the creatures were more horrible than could be dreamed. The bulbous object on their bodies just might be a head, Cordovir decided, even though it was unlike any head he had ever seen. But in the middle of that head, instead of a smooth, characterful surface was a raised ridge. Two round indentures were on either side of it, and two more knobs on either side of that. And in the lower half of the head – if such it was – a pale, reddish slash ran across. Cordovir supposed this might be considered a mouth, with some stretching of the imagination.

Nor was this all, Cordovir observed. The things were so constructed as to show the presence of bone. When they moved their limbs, it wasn't a smooth, flowing gesture, the fluid motion of human beings. Rather, it was the jerky snap of a tree limb.

'God above,' Gilrig, an intermediate-age male, gasped. 'We should kill them and put them out of their misery.' Other men seemed to feel the same way, and the villagers flowed forward.

'Wait!' one of the youngsters shouted. 'Let's communicate with them, if such is possible! They might still be moral beings. The Outside is wide, remember, and anything is possible.'

Cordovir argued for immediate extermination, but the villagers stopped and discussed it among themselves. Hum, with characteristic bravado, flowed up to the thing on the ground.

'Hello,' Hum said.

The thing said something.

'I can't understand it,' Hum said, and started to crawl back. The creature waved its jointed tentacles – if they were tentacles – and motioned at one of the suns. He made a sound.

'Yes, it is warm, isn't it?' Hum said cheerfully.

The creature pointed at the ground, and made another sound.

'We haven't had especially good crops this year,' Hum said conversationally.

The creature pointed at itself and made a sound.

'I agree,' Hum said. 'You're as ugly as sin.'

Presently the villagers grew hungry and crawled back to the village. Hum stayed and listened to the things making noises at him, and Cordovir waited nervously for Hum.

'You know,' Hum said, after he rejoined Cordovir, 'I think they want to learn our language. Or want me to learn theirs.'

'Don't do it!' Cordovir said, glimpsing the misty edge of a great evil.

'I believe I will,' Hum murmured. Together they climbed the cliffs back to the village.

That afternoon Cordovir went to the surplus female pen and formally asked a young woman if she would reign in his house for twenty-five days. Naturally, the woman accepted gratefully.

On the way home, Cordovir met Hum, going to the pen.

'Just killed my wife,' Hum said, superfluously, since why else would he be going to the surplus female stock?

'Are you going back to the creatures tomorrow?' Cordovir asked.

'I might,' Hum answered, 'if nothing new presents itself.'

'The thing to find out is if they are moral beings or monsters.'

'Right!' Hum said, and slithered on.

There was a Gathering that evening, after supper. All the villagers agreed that the things were non-human. Cordovir argued strenuously that their very appearance belied any possibility of humanity. Nothing so hideous could have moral standards, a sense of right and wrong, and above all, a notion of truth.

The young men didn't agree, probably because there had been a dearth of new things recently. They pointed out that the metal object was obviously a product of intelligence. Intelligence axiomatically means standards of differentiation. Differentiation implies right and wrong.

It was a delicious argument. Olgolel contradicted Arast and was killed by him. Mavrt, in an unusual fit of anger for so placid an individual, killed the three Holian brothers and was himself killed by Hum, who was feeling pettish. Even the surplus females could be heard arguing about it, in their pen in a corner of the village.

Weary and happy, the villagers went to sleep.

The next few weeks saw no end of the argument. Life went on much as usual, though. The women went out in the morning, gathered food, prepared it, and laid eggs. The eggs were taken to the surplus females to be hatched. As usual, about eight females were hatched to every male. On the twenty-fifth day of each marriage, or a little earlier, each man killed his woman and took another.

The males went down to the ship to listen to Hum learning the language; then, when that grew boring, they returned to their customary wandering through hills and forests, looking for new things.

The alien monsters stayed close to their ship, coming out only when Hum was there.

Twenty-four days after the arrival of the non-humans, Hum announced that he could communicate with them, after a fashion.

'They say they come from far away,' Hum told the village that evening. 'They say that they are bisexual, like us, and that they are humans, like us. They say there are reasons for their different appearance, but I couldn't understand that part of it.'

'If we accept them as humans,' Mishill said, 'then everything they say is true.'

The rest of the villagers shook in agreement.

'They say that they don't want to disturb our life, but would be very interested in observing it. They want to come to the village and look around.'

'I see no reason why not,' one of the younger men said.

'No!' Cordovir shouted. 'You are letting in evil. These monsters are insidious. I believe that they are capable of – telling an untruth.' The other elders agreed, but when pressed, Cordovir had no proof to back up this vicious accusation.

'After all,' Sil pointed out, 'just because they look like monsters, you can't take it for granted that they think like monsters as well.'

'I can,' Cordovir said, but he was outvoted.

Hum went on. 'They have offered me – or us, I'm not sure which – various metal objects which they say will do various things. I ignored this breach of etiquette, since I considered they didn't know any better.'

Cordovir nodded. The youngster was growing up. He was showing, at long last, that he had some manners.

'They want to come to the village tomorrow.'

'No!' Cordovir shouted, but the vote was against him.

'Oh, by the way,' Hum said, as the meeting was break- ing up. 'They have several females among them. The ones with the very red mouths are females. It will be inter- esting to see how the males kill them. Tomorrow is the twenty-fifth day since they came.'

The next day the things came to the village, crawling slowly and laboriously over the cliffs. The villagers were able to observe the extreme brittleness of their limbs, the terrible awkwardness of their motions.

'No beauty whatsoever,' Cordovir muttered. 'And they all look alike.'

In the village the things acted without any decency. They crawled into huts and out of huts. They jabbered at the surplus female pen. They picked up eggs and examined them. They peered at the villagers through black things and shiny things.

In mid-afternoon, Rantan, an elder, decided it was about time he killed his woman. So he pushed the thing who was examining his hut aside and smashed his female to death.

Instantly, two of the things started jabbering at each other, hurrying out of the hut.

One had the red mouth of a female.

'He must have remembered it was time to kill his own woman,' Hum observed. The villagers waited, but nothing happened.

'Perhaps,' Rantan said, 'perhaps he would like someone to kill her for him. It might be the custom of their land.'

Without further ado Rantan slashed down the female with his tail.

The male creature made a terrible noise and pointed a metal stick at Rantan. Rantan collapsed, dead.

'That's odd,' Mishill said. 'I wonder if that denotes disapproval?'

The things from the metal object – eight of them – were in a tight little circle. One was holding the dead female, and the rest were pointing the metal sticks on all sides. Hum went up and asked them what was wrong.

'I don't understand,' Hum said, after he spoke with them. 'They used words I haven't learned. But I gather that their emotion is one of reproach.'

The monsters were backing away. Another villager, deciding it was about time, killed his wife who was standing in a doorway. The group of monsters stopped and jabbered at each other. Then they motioned to Hum.

Hum's body motion was incredulous after he had talked with them.

'If I understood right,' Hum said, 'they are ordering us not to kill any more of our women.'

'What!' Cordovir and a dozen others shouted.

'I'll ask them again.' Hum went back into conference with the monsters who were waving metal sticks in their tentacles.

'That's right,' Hum said. Without further preamble he flipped his tail, throwing one of the monsters across the village square. Immediately the others began to point their sticks while retreating rapidly.

After they were gone, the villagers found that seventeen males were dead. Hum, for some reason, had been missed.

'Now will you believe me?' Cordovir shouted. 'The creatures told a *deliberate untruth*. They said they wouldn't molest us and then they proceed to kill seventeen of us. Not only an amoral act – but a *concerted death effort!*'

It was almost past human understanding.

'A deliberate untruth!' Cordovir shouted the blasphemy, sick with loathing. Men rarely discussed the possibility of anyone telling an untruth.

The villagers were beside themselves with anger and revulsion, once they realized the full concept of an *untruthful* creature. And, added to that was the monsters' concerted death effort.

It was like the most horrible nightmare come true. Suddenly it became apparent that these creatures didn't kill females. Undoubtedly they allowed them to spawn unhampered. The thought of that was enough to make a strong man retch.

The surplus females broke out of their pens and, joined by the wives, demanded to know what was happening. When they were told, they were twice as indignant as the men, such being the nature of women.

'Kill them!' the surplus females roared. 'Don't let them change our ways! Don't let them introduce immorality!'

'It's true,' Hiram said sadly. 'I should have guessed it.'

'They must be killed at once,' a female shouted. Being surplus, she had no name at present, but she made up for that in blazing personality.

'We women desire only to live moral, decent lives, hatching eggs in the pen until our time of marriage comes. And then twenty-five ecstatic days! How could we desire more? These monsters will destroy our way of life. They will make us as terrible as they.'

'Now do you understand?' Cordovir screamed at the men. 'I warned you, I presented it to you, and you ignored me. Young men must listen to old men in time of crisis.' In this rage he killed two youngsters with a blow of his tail. The villagers applauded.

'Drive them out,' Cordovir shouted. 'Before they corrupt us!'

All the females rushed off to kill the monsters.

'They have death-sticks,' Hum observed. 'Do the females know?'

'I don't believe so,' Cordovir said. He was completely calm now. 'You'd better go and tell them.'

'I'm tired,' Hum said sulkily. 'I've been translating. Why don't you go?'

'Oh, let's both go,' Cordovir said, bored with the youngster's adolescent moodiness. Accompanied by half the villagers they hurried off after the females.

They overtook them on the edge of the cliff that overlooked the object. Hum explained the death-sticks while Cordovir considered the problem.

'Roll stones on them!' he told the females. 'Perhaps you can break the metal of the object.'

The females started rolling stones down the cliffs with great energy. Some bounced off the metal of the object. Immediately, lines of red fire came from the object and females were killed. The ground shook.

'Let's move back!' Cordovir said. 'The females have it well in hand, and this shaky ground makes me giddy.'

Together with the rest of the males they moved to a safe distance and watched the action.

Women were dying right and left, but they were reinforced by women of other villages who had heard of the menace. They were fighting for their homes now, their rights, and they were fiercer than a man could ever be. The object was throwing fire all over the cliff, but the fire helped dislodge more stones which rained down on the thing. Finally, big fires came out of one end of the metal object.

A landslide started, and the object got into the air just in time. It barely missed a mountain; then it climbed steadily, until it was a little black speck against the larger sun. And then it was gone.

That evening, it was discovered that fifty-three females had been killed. This was fortunate since it helped keep down the surplus female population. The problem would become even more acute now, since seventeen males were gone in a single lump.

Cordovir was feeling exceedingly proud of himself. His wife had been gloriously killed in the fighting, but he took another at once.

'We had better kill our wives sooner than every twenty-five days for a while,' he said at the evening Gathering. 'Just until things get back to normal.'

The surviving females, back in the pen, heard him and applauded wildly.

'I wonder where the things have gone,' Hum said, offering the question to the Gathering.

'Probably away to enslave some defenceless race,' Cordovir said.

'Not necessarily,' Mishill put in and the evening argument was on.

Cost of Living

Carrin decided that he could trace his present mood to Miller's suicide last week. But the knowledge didn't help him get rid of the vague, formless fears in the back of his mind. It was foolish. Miller's suicide didn't concern him.

But why had that fat, jovial man killed himself? Miller had had everything to live for – wife, kids, good job, and all the marvellous luxuries of the age. Why had he done it?

'Good morning, dear!' Carrin's wife said as he sat down at the breakfast table.

'Morning, honey! Morning, Billy!'

His son grunted something.

You just couldn't tell about people, Carrin decided, and dialled his breakfast. The meal was gracefully prepared and served by the new Avignon Electric Auto-cook.

His mood persisted, annoyingly enough since Carrin wanted to be in top form this morning. It was his day off, and the Avignon Electric finance man was coming. This was an important day.

He walked to the door with his son.

'Have a good day, Billy!'

His son nodded, shifted his books and started to school without answering. Carrin wondered if something was bothering him, too. He hoped not. One worrier in the family was plenty.

'See you later, honey.' He kissed his wife as she left to go shopping.

At any rate, he thought, watching her go down the walk, she's happy. He wondered how much she'd spend at the A. E. store.

Checking his watch, he found that he had half an hour before the A. E. finance man was due. The best way to get rid of a bad mood was to drown it, he told himself, and headed for the shower.

The shower-room was a glittering plastic wonder, and the sheer luxury of it eased Carrin's mind. He threw his clothes into the A. E. automatic Kleen-presser, and adjusted the shower spray to a notch above 'brisk'. The five-degrees-above-skin-temperature water beat against his thin white body. Delightful! And then a relaxing rub-dry in the A. E. Auto-towel.

Wonderful, he thought, as the towel stretched and kneaded his stringy muscles. And it should be wonderful, he reminded himself. The A. E. Auto-towel with shaving attachments had cost three hundred and thirteen dollars, plus tax.

But worth every penny of it, he decided, as the A. E. shaver came out of a corner and whisked off his rudimentary stubble. After all, what good was life if you couldn't enjoy the luxuries?

His skin tingled when he switched off the Auto-towel. He should have been feeling wonderful, but he wasn't. Miller's suicide kept nagging at his mind, destroying the peace of his day off.

Was there anything else bothering him? Certainly

there was nothing wrong with the house. His papers were in order for the finance man.

'Have I forgotten something?' he asked out loud.

'The Avignon Electric finance man will be here in fifteen minutes,' his A. E. bathroom Wall-reminder whispered.

'I know that. Is there anything else?'

The Wall-reminder reeled off its memorized data – a vast amount of minutiae about watering the lawn, having the Jet-lash checked, buying lamb chops for Monday, and the like. Things he still hadn't found time for.

'All right, that's enough.' He allowed the A. E. Auto-dresser to dress him, skilfully draping a new selection of fabrics over his bony frame. A whiff of fashionable masculine perfume finished him and he went into the living-room, threading his way between the appliances that lined the walls.

A quick inspection of the dials on the wall assured him that the house was in order. The breakfast dishes had been sanitized and stacked, the house had been cleaned, dusted, polished, his wife's garments had been hung up, his son's model rocket-ships had been put back in the closet.

'Stop worrying, you hypochondriac!' he told himself angrily.

The door announced, 'Mr Pathis from Avignon Finance is here.'

Carrin started to tell the door to open, when he noticed the Automatic Bartender.

Good God, why hadn't he thought of it?

The Automatic Bartender was manufactured by Castile Motors. He had bought it in a weak moment. A.E.

wouldn't think very highly of that, since they sold their own brand.

He wheeled the bartender into the kitchen, and told the door to open.

'A very good day to you, sir!' Mr Pathis said.

Pathis was a tall, imposing man, dressed in a conservative tweed drape. His eyes had the crinkled corners of a man who laughs frequently. He beamed broadly and shook Carrin's hand, looking around the crowded living-room.

'A beautiful place you have here, sir. Beautiful! As a matter of fact, I don't think I'll be overstepping the company's code to inform you that yours is the nicest interior in this section.'

Carrin felt a sudden glow of pride at that, thinking of the rows of identical houses, on this block and the next, and the one after that.

'Now then, is everything functioning properly?' Mr Pathis asked, setting his brief-case on a chair. 'Everything in order?'

'Oh, yes!' Carrin said enthusiastically. 'Avignon Electric never goes out of whack.'

'The phono all right? Changes records for the full seventeen hours?'

'It certainly does,' Carrin said. He hadn't had a chance to try out the phono, but it was a beautiful piece of furniture.

'The Solido-projector all right? Enjoying the programmes?'

'Absolutely perfect reception.' He had watched a programme just last month, and it had been startlingly life-like.

'How about the kitchen? Auto-cook in order? Recipe-master still knocking 'em out?'

'Marvellous stuff. Simply marvellous.'

Mr Pathis went on to inquire about his refrigerator, his vacuum cleaner, his car, his helicopter, his subterranean swimming pool, and the hundreds of other items Carrin had bought from Avignon Electric.

'Everything is swell,' Carrin said, a trifle untruthfully since he hadn't unpacked every item yet. 'Just wonderful.'

'I'm so glad,' Mr Pathis said, leaning back with a sigh of relief. 'You have no idea how hard we try to satisfy our customers. If a product isn't right, back it comes, no questions asked. We believe in pleasing our customers.'

'I certainly appreciate it, Mr Pathis.'

Carrin hoped the A. E. man wouldn't ask to see the kitchen. He visualized the Castile Motors Bartender in there, like a porcupine in a dog show.

'I'm proud to say that most of the people in this neighbourhood buy from us,' Mr Pathis was saying. 'We're a solid firm.'

'Was Mr Miller a customer of yours?' Carrin asked.

'That fellow who killed himself?' Pathis frowned briefly. 'He was, as a matter of fact. That amazed me, sir, absolutely amazed me. Why, just last month the fellow bought a brand-new Jet-lash from me, capable of doing three hundred and fifty miles an hour on a straight-away. He was as happy as a kid over it, and then to go and do a thing like that! Of course, the Jet-lash brought up his debt a little.'

'Of course.'

'But what did that matter? He had every luxury in the world. And then he went and hanged himself.'

'Hanged himself?'

'Yes,' Pathis said, the frown coming back. 'Every modern convenience in his house, and he hanged himself with a piece of rope. Probably unbalanced for a long time.'

The frown slid off his face, and the customary smile replaced it. 'But enough of that! Let's talk about you!'

The smile widened as Pathis opened his brief-case. 'Now, then, your account. You owe us two hundred and three thousand dollars and twenty-nine cents, Mr Carrin, as of your last purchase. Right?'

'Right,' Carrin said, remembering the amount from his own papers. 'Here's my instalment.'

He handed Pathis an envelope, which the man checked and put in his pocket.

'Fine. Now you know, Mr Carrin, that you won't live long enough to pay us the full two hundred thousand, don't you?'

'No, I don't suppose I will,' Carrin said soberly.

He was only thirty-nine, with a full hundred years of life before him, thanks to the marvels of medical science. But at a salary of three thousand a year, he still couldn't pay it all off and have enough to support a family on at the same time.

'Of course, we would not want to deprive you of necessities. To say nothing of the terrific items that are coming out next year. Things you wouldn't want to miss, sir!'

Mr Carrin nodded. Certainly he wanted new items.

'Well, suppose we make the customary arrangement.

If you will just sign over your son's earnings for the first thirty years of his adult life, we can easily arrange credit for you.'

Mr Pathis whipped the papers out of his brief-case and spread them in front of Carrin.

'If you'll just sign here, sir.'

'Well,' Carrin said, 'I'm not sure. I'd like to give the boy a start in life, not saddle him with—'

'But my dear sir,' Pathis interposed, 'this is for your son as well. He lives here, doesn't he? He has a right to enjoy the luxuries, the marvels of science.'

'Sure,' Carrin said. 'Only—'

'Why, sir, to-day the average man is living like a king. A hundred years ago the richest man in the world couldn't buy what any ordinary citizen possesses at present. You mustn't look upon it as a debt. It's an investment.'

'That's true,' Carrin said dubiously.

He thought about his son and his rocket-ship models, his star charts, his maps. Would it be right? he asked himself.

'What's wrong?' Pathis asked cheerfully.

'Well, I was just wondering,' Carrin said. 'Signing over my son's earnings – you don't think I'm getting in a little too deep, do you?'

'Too deep? My dear sir!' Pathis exploded into laughter. 'Do you know Mellon down the block? Well, don't say I said it, but he's already mortgaged his grandchildren's salary for their full life-expectancy. And he doesn't have half the goods he's made up his mind to own. We'll work out something for him. Service to the customer is our job and we know it well.'

Carrin wavered visibly.

'And after you're gone, sir, they'll all belong to your son.'

That was true, Carrin thought. His son would have all the marvellous things that filled the house. And after all, it was only thirty years out of a life expectancy of a hundred and fifty.

He signed with a flourish.

'Excellent!' Pathis said. 'And by the way, has your home got an A. E. Master-operator?'

It hadn't. Pathis explained that a Master-operator was new this year, a stupendous advance in scientific engineering. It was designed to take all the functions of housecleaning and cooking, without its owner having to lift a finger.

'Instead of running around all day, pushing half a dozen different buttons, with the Master-operator, all you have to do is push *one*! A remarkable achievement!'

Since it was only five hundred and thirty-five dollars, Carrin signed for one, having it added to his son's debt.

Right's right, he thought, walking Pathis to the door. This house will be Billy's some day. His and his wife's. They certainly will want everything up-to-date.

Just one button, he thought. That *would* be a time-saver!

After Pathis left, Carrin sat back in an adjustable chair and turned on the solido. After twisting the Ezidial, he discovered that there was nothing he wanted to see. He tilted back the chair and took a nap.

The something on his mind was still bothering him.

'Hello, darling!' He awoke to find his wife was home. She kissed him on the ear. 'Look!'

She had bought an A. E. Sexitizer-négligée. He was pleasantly surprised that that was all she had bought. Usually, Leela returned from shopping laden down.

'It's lovely,' he said.

She bent over for a kiss, then giggled – a habit he knew she had picked up from the latest popular solido star. He wished she hadn't.

'Going to dial supper,' she said, and went to the kitchen. Carrin smiled, thinking that soon she would be able to dial the meals without moving out of the living-room. He settled back in his chair, and his son walked in.

'How's it going, Son?' he asked heartily.

'All right,' Billy answered listlessly.

'What'sa matter, Son?' The boy stared at his feet, not answering. 'Come on, tell Dad what's the trouble!'

Billy sat down on a packing-case and put his chin in his hands. He looked thoughtfully at his father.

'Dad, could I be a Master Repairman if I wanted to be?'

Mr Carrin smiled at the question. Billy alternated between wanting to be a Master Repairman and a rocket pilot. The repairmen were the elite. It was their job to fix the automatic repair machines. The repair machines could fix just about anything, but you couldn't have a machine fix the machine that fixed the machine. That was where the Master Repairmen came in.

But it was a highly competitive field and only a very few of the best brains were able to get their degrees. And, although the boy was bright, he didn't seem to have an engineering bent.

'It's possible, Son. Anything is possible.'

'But is it possible for me?'

'I don't know,' Carrin answered, as honestly as he could.

'Well, I don't want to be a Master Repairman anyway,' the boy said, seeing that the answer was no. 'I want to be a space pilot.'

'A space pilot, Billy?' Leela asked, coming in to the room. 'But there aren't any.'

'Yes, there are,' Billy argued. 'We were told in school that the government is going to send some men to Mars.'

'They've been saying that for a hundred years,' Carrin said, 'and they still haven't got around to doing it.'

'They will this time.'

'Why would you want to go to Mars?' Leela asked, winking at Carrin. 'There are no pretty girls on Mars.'

'I'm not interested in girls. I just want to go to Mars.'

'You wouldn't like it, honey,' Leela said. 'It's a nasty old place with no air.'

'It's got some air. I'd like to go there,' the boy insisted sullenly. 'I don't like it here.'

'What's that?' Carrin asked, sitting up straight. 'Is there anything you haven't got? Anything you want?'

'No, sir. I've got everything I want.' Whenever his son called him 'sir', Carrin knew that something was wrong.

'Look, Son, when I was your age I wanted to go to Mars, too. I wanted to do romantic things. I even wanted to be a Master Repairman.'

'Then why didn't you?'

'Well, I grew up. I realized that there were more important things. First I had to pay off the debt my father had left me, and then I met your mother—'

Leela giggled.

'– and I wanted a home of my own. It'll be the same with you. You'll pay off your debt and get married, the same as the rest of us.'

Billy was silent for a while. Then he brushed his dark hair – straight, like his father's – back from his forehead and wet his lips.

'How come I have debts, sir?'

Carrin explained carefully. About the things a family needed for civilized living, and the cost of those items. How they had to be paid. How it was customary for a son to take on a part of his parent's debt, when he came of age.

Billy's silence annoyed him. It was almost as if the boy were reproaching him, after he had slaved for years to give the ungrateful whelp every luxury.

'Son,' he said harshly, 'have you studied history in school? Good! Then you know how it was in the past. Wars. How would you like to get blown up in a war?'

The boy didn't answer.

'Or how would you like to break your back for eight hours a day, doing work a machine should handle? Or be hungry all the time? Or cold, with the rain beating down on you, and no place to sleep?'

He paused for a response, got none and went on. 'You live in the most fortunate age mankind has ever known. You are surrounded by every wonder of art and science. The finest music, the greatest books and art, all at your fingertips. All you have to do is push a button.' He shifted to a kindlier tone. 'Well, what are you thinking?'

'I was just wondering how I could go to Mars,' the boy said. 'With the debt, I mean. I don't suppose I could get away from that.'

'Of course not.'

'Unless I stowed away on a rocket.'

'But you wouldn't do that.'

'No, of course not,' the boy said, but his tone lacked conviction.

'You'll stay here and marry a very nice girl,' Leela told him.

'Sure I will,' Billy said. 'Sure.' He grinned suddenly. 'I didn't mean any of that stuff about going to Mars. I really didn't.'

'I'm glad of that,' Leela answered.

'Just forget I mentioned it,' Billy said, smiling stiffly. He stood up and raced upstairs.

'Probably gone to play with his rockets,' Leela said. 'He's such a little devil.'

The Carrins ate a quiet supper, and then it was time for Mr Carrin to go to work. He was on night shift this month. He kissed his wife good-bye, climbed into his Jet-lash and roared to the factory. The automatic gates recognized him and opened. He parked and walked in.

Automatic lathes, automatic presses – everything was automatic. The factory was huge and bright, and the machines hummed softly to themselves, doing their job and doing it well.

Carrin walked to the end of the automatic washing-machine assembly line, to relieve the man there.

'Everything all right?' he asked.

'Sure,' the man said. 'Haven't had a bad one all year. These new models here have built-in voices. They don't light up like the old ones.'

Carrin sat down where the man had sat and waited

for the first washing-machine to come through. His job was the soul of simplicity. He just sat there and the machines went by him. He pressed a button on them and found out if they were all right. They always were. After passing him, the washing-machines went to the packaging section.

The first one slid by on the long slide of rollers. He pressed the starting button on the side.

'Ready for the wash,' the washing-machine said.

Carrin pressed the release and let it go by.

That boy of his, Carrin thought. Would he grow up and face his responsibilities? Would he mature and take his place in society? Carrin doubted it. The boy was a born rebel. If anyone got to Mars, it would be his kid.

But the thought didn't especially disturb him.

'Ready for the wash.' Another machine went by.

Carrin remembered something about Miller. The jovial man had always been talking about the planets, always kidding about going off somewhere and roughing it. He hadn't, though. He had committed suicide.

'Ready for the wash.'

Carrin had eight hours in front of him, and he loosened his belt to prepare for it. Eight hours of pushing buttons and listening to a machine announce its readiness.

'Ready for the wash.'

He pressed the release.

'Ready for the wash.'

Carrin's mind strayed from the job, which didn't need much attention in any case. He realized now what had been bothering him.

He didn't enjoy pushing buttons.

The Altar

With a sprightly gait, Mr Slater walked down Maple Street towards the station. There was a little bounce to his step this morning, and a smile on his clean-shaven substantial face. It was such a glorious spring morning.

Mr Slater hummed a tune to himself, glad of the seven-block walk to the railroad station. Although the distance had been a bother all winter, weather like this made up for it. It was a pleasure to be alive, a joy to be commuting.

Just then he was stopped by a man in a light-blue top-coat.

'Pardon me, sir,' the man said. 'Could you direct me to the Altar of Baz-Matain?'

Mr Slater, still full of the beauties of spring, tried to think. 'Baz-Matain? I don't think – the *Altar* of Baz-Matain, you say?'

'That's right,' the stranger said, with an apologetic little smile. He was unusually tall, and he had a dark, thin face. Mr Slater decided it was a foreign-looking face.

'Terribly sorry,' Mr Slater said, after a moment's thought. 'I don't believe I ever heard of it.'

'Thanks anyhow,' the dark man said, nodded pleasantly and walked off towards the centre of town. Mr Slater continued to the station.

After the conductor punched his ticket, Mr Slater thought of the incident. *Baz-Matain*, he repeated to himself as the train sped through the misty, ragged fields of New Jersey. *Baz-Matain*. Mr Slater decided that the foreign-looking man must have been mistaken. North Ambrose, New Jersey, was a small town; small enough for a resident to know every street in it, every house or store. Especially a resident of almost twenty years' standing, like Mr Slater.

Half-way through the office day, Mr Slater found himself tapping a pencil against the glass top of his desk, thinking of the man in the light-blue top-coat. A foreign-looking fellow was an oddity in North Ambrose, a quiet, refined, settled suburb. The North Ambrose men wore good business suits and carried lean brown suitcases; some were fat and some were thin, but anyone in North Ambrose might have been taken for anyone else's brother.

Mr Slater didn't think of it any more. He finished his day, took the tube to Hoboken, the train to North Ambrose, and finally started the walk to his house.

On the way he passed the man again.

'I found it,' the stranger said. 'It wasn't easy, but I found it.'

'Where was it?' Mr Slater asked, stopping.

'Right beside the Temple of Dark Mysteries of Isis,' the stranger said. 'Stupid of me. I should have asked for that in the first place. I knew it was here, but it never occurred to me—'

'The temple of what?' Mr Slater asked.

'Dark Mysteries of Isis,' the dark man said. 'Not competitors, really. Seers and warlocks, fertility cycles and the like. Never come near *our* province.'

'I see,' Mr Slater said, looking at the stranger closely in the early spring twilight. 'The reason I asked, I've lived in this town a number of years, and I don't believe I ever heard—'

'Say!' the man exclaimed, glancing at his watch. 'Didn't realize how late it was. I'll be holding up the ceremony if I don't hurry.' And with a friendly wave of his hand, he hurried off.

Mr Slater walked slowly home, thinking. *Altar of Baz-Matain. Dark Mysteries of Isis.* They sounded like cults. Could there be such places in his town? It seemed impossible. No one would rent to people like that.

After supper, Mr Slater consulted the telephone book. But there was no listing for Baz-Matain, or for the Temple of Dark Mysteries of Isis. Information wasn't able to supply them either.

'Odd,' he mused. Later, he told his wife about the two meetings with the foreign man.

'Well,' she said, pulling her house robe closer around her, 'no one's going to start any cults in this town. The Better Business Bureau wouldn't allow it. To say nothing of the Women's Club, or the P. T. A.'

Mr Slater agreed. The stranger must have had the wrong town. Perhaps the cults were in South Ambrose, a neighbouring town with several bars and a picture house, and a distinctly undesirable element in its population.

The next morning was Friday. Mr Slater looked for the stranger, but all he saw were his homogeneous fellow commuters. It was the same on the way back. Evidently the fellow had visited the Altar and left. Or he had taken up duties there at hours which didn't coincide with Mr Slater's commuting hours.

Monday morning Mr Slater left his house a few minutes late and was hurrying to catch his train. Ahead he saw the blue top-coat.

'Hello there!' Mr Slater called.

'Why hello!' the dark man said, his thin face breaking into a smile. 'I was wondering when we would bump into each other again.'

'So was I,' Mr Slater said, showing his paces. The stranger was strolling along evidently enjoying the magnificent weather. Mr Slater knew that he was going to miss his train.

'And how are things at the Altar?' Mr Slater asked.

'So-so,' the man said, his hands clasped behind his back. 'To tell you the truth, we're having a bit of trouble.'

'Oh?' Mr Slater asked.

'Yes,' the dark man said, his face stern. 'Old Atherhotep, the mayor, is threatening to revoke our licence in North Ambrose. Says we aren't fulfilling our charter. But I ask you, how can we? What with the Dionysus-Africanus set across the street grabbing everyone likely, and the Papa Legba-Damballa combine two doors down, taking even the unlikely ones – well, what can you do?'

'It doesn't sound too good,' Mr Slater agreed.

'That's not all,' the stranger said. 'Our high priest is threatening to leave if we don't get some action. He's a seventh degree adept, and Brahma alone knows where we'd get another.'

'Mmm,' Mr Slater murmured.

'That's what *I'm* here for, though,' the stranger said. 'If they're going to use sharp business practices, I'll go them one better. I'm the new business manager, you know.'

'Oh?' Mr Slater said, surprised. 'Are you re-organizing?'

'In a way,' the stranger told him. 'You see, it's like this—' Just then a short, plump man hurried up and seized the dark man by the sleeve of the blue top-coat.

'Elor,' he panted. 'I miscalculated the date. It's *this* Monday. Today, not next week.'

'Damn!' the dark man said succinctly. 'You'll have to excuse me,' he said to Mr Slater. 'This is rather urgent.' He hurried away with the short man.

Mr Slater was half an hour late for work that morning, but he didn't care. It was all pretty obvious, he thought, sitting at his desk. A group of cults was springing up in North Ambrose, vying for congregations. And the mayor, instead of getting rid of them, was doing nothing. Perhaps he was even taking bribes.

Mr Slater tapped his pencil against his glass-topped desk. How was it possible? Nothing could be hidden in North Ambrose. It was such a little town. Mr Slater knew a good percentage of the inhabitants by their first names. How could something like this go on unnoticed?

Angrily, he reached for the telephone.

Information was unable to supply him with the numbers of Dionysus-Africanus, Papa Legba or Damballa. The mayor of North Ambrose, he was informed, was not Atherhotep, but a man named Miller. Mr Slater telephoned him.

The conversation was far from satisfying. The mayor insisted that he knew every business in the town, every church, every lodge. And if there were any cults – which there weren't – he would know of them too.

'You have been deluded, my good man,' Mayor Miller said, a little too pompously to suit Mr Slater. 'There are no people by those names in this town, no such organizations. We would never allow them in.'

Mr Slater thought this over carefully on the way home. As he stepped off the train platform he saw Elor, hurrying across Oak Street with short, rapid steps.

Elor stopped when Mr Slater called to him.

'Really can't stay,' he said cheerfully. 'The ceremony begins soon, and I must be there. It was that fool Ligian's fault.'

Ligian, Mr Slater decided, would be the plump man who had stopped Elor in the morning.

'He's so careless,' Elor went on. 'Can you imagine a competent astrologer making a mistake of a week in the conjugation of Saturn with Scorpio? No matter. We hold the ceremony tonight, short-handed or not.'

'Could I come?' Mr Slater asked, without hesitation. 'I mean, if you're short-handed—'

'Well,' Elor mused. 'It's unprecedented.'

'I'd really like to,' Mr Slater said, seeing a chance to get to the bottom of the mystery.

'I really don't think it's fair to you,' Elor went on, his thin, dark face thoughtful. 'Without preparation and all—'

'I'll be all right,' Mr Slater insisted. He would really have something to dump in the mayor's lap if this worked! 'I really want to go. You've got me quite excited about it.'

'All right,' Elor said. 'We'd better hurry.'

They walked down Oak Street, towards the centre of town. Then, just as they reached the first stores, Elor turned. He led Mr Slater two blocks over and a block down, and then retraced a block. After that he headed back toward the railroad station.

It was getting quite dark.

'Isn't there a simpler way?' Mr Slater asked.

'Oh, no,' Elor said. 'This is the most direct. If you knew the roundabout way I came the first time—'

They walked on, backtracking blocks, circling, re-crossing streets they had already passed, going back and forth over the town Mr Slater knew so well.

But as it grew darker, and as they approached familiar streets from unfamiliar directions, Mr Slater became just a trifle confused. He knew where he was, of course, but the constant circling had thrown him off.

How very strange, he thought. One can get lost in one's own town, even after living there almost twenty years.

Mr Slater tried to place what street they were on without looking at the signpost, and then they made another unexpected turn. He had just made up his mind that they were backtracking on Walnut Lane, when he found that he couldn't remember the next cross street. As they passed the corner, he looked at the sign.

It read: Left Orifice.

Mr Slater couldn't remember any street in North Ambrose called Left Orifice.

There were no streetlights on it, and Mr Slater found that he didn't recognize any of the stores. That was strange, because he thought he knew the little business section of North Ambrose very well. It gave him quite a start when they passed one squat black building on which there was a dimly-lighted sign.

The sign read: *Temple of the Dark Mysteries of Isis*.

'They're pretty quiet in there tonight, eh?' Elor said, following Mr Slater's glance towards the building. 'We'd better hurry.' He walked faster, allowing Mr Slater no time to ask questions.

The buildings became stranger and stranger as they walked down the dim street. They were of all shapes and sizes, some new and glistening, others ancient and decayed. Mr Slater couldn't imagine any section in North Ambrose like this. Was there a town within the town? Could there be a North Ambrose by night that the day-time inhabitants knew nothing of? A North Ambrose approached only by devious turns through familiar streets?

'Phallic rites in there,' Elor said, indicating a tall, slender building. Beside it was a twisted, sagging hulk of a place.

'That's Damballa's place,' Elor said, pointing at it.

Towards the end of the street was a white building. It was quite long, and built low to the ground. Mr Slater hadn't time to examine it, because Elor had his arm and was hurrying him in the door.

'I really must become more prompt,' Elor muttered half to himself.

Once inside, it was totally dark. Mr Slater could feel movement around him, and then he made out a tiny white light. Elor guided him towards it, saying in friendly tones, 'You've really helped me out of a jam.'

'Have you got it?' a thin voice asked from beside the light. Mr Slater began to make out shapes. As his eyes became more accustomed to the gloom, he could see a tiny, gnarled old man in front of the light.

The old man was holding an unusually long knife.

'Of course,' Elor said. 'And he was willing, too.'

The white light was suspended over a stone altar, Mr Slater realized. In a single reflex action he turned to run, but Elor's hand was tight on his arm.

'You can't leave us now,' Elor said gently. 'We're ready to begin.'

And then there were other hands on Mr Slater, many of them, pulling him steadily towards the Altar.

Keep Your Shape

Pid the Pilot slowed the ship almost to a standstill, and peered anxiously at the green planet below.

Even without instruments, there was no mistaking it. Third from its sun, it was the only planet in this system capable of sustaining life. Peacefully it swam beneath its gauze of clouds.

It looked very innocent. And yet, twenty previous Grom expeditions had set out to prepare this planet for invasion – and vanished utterly, without a word.

Pid hesitated only a moment, before starting irrevocably down. There was no point in hovering and worrying. He and his two crewmen were as ready now as they would ever be. Their compact Displacers were stored in body pouches, inactive but ready.

Pid wanted to say something to his crew, but wasn't sure how to put it.

The crew waited. Ilg the Radioman had sent the final message to the Grom planet. Ger the Detector read sixteen dials at once, and reported, 'No sign of alien activity.' His body surfaces flowed carelessly.

Noticing the flow, Pid knew what to say to his crew. Ever since they had left Grom, shape-discipline had been disgustingly lax. The Invasion Chief had warned him; but still, he had to do something about it. It was his duty, since lower castes such as Radiomen and Detectors were notoriously prone to Shapelessness.

'A lot of hopes are resting on this expedition,' he began slowly. 'We're a long way from home now.'

Ger the Detector nodded. Ilg the Radioman flowed out of his prescribed shape and moulded himself comfortably to a wall.

'However,' Pid said sternly, 'distance is no excuse for promiscuous Shapelessness.'

Ilg flowed hastily back into proper Radioman's shape.

'Exotic forms will undoubtedly be called for,' Pid went on. 'And for that we have a special dispensation. But remember – any shape not assumed strictly in the line of duty is a foul, lawless device of The Shapeless One!'

Ger's body surfaces abruptly stopped flowing.

'That's all,' Pid said, and flowed into his controls. The ship started down, so smoothly co-ordinated that Pid felt a glow of pride.

They were good workers, he decided. He just couldn't expect them to be as shape-conscious as a high-caste Pilot. Even the Invasion Chief had told him that.

'Pid,' the Invasion Chief had said at their last interview, 'we need this planet desperately.'

'Yes, sir,' Pid had said, standing at full attention, never quivering from Optimum Pilot's Shape.

'One of you,' the Chief said heavily, 'must get through and set up a Displacer near an atomic power source. The army will be standing by at this end, ready to step through.'

'We'll do it, sir,' Pid said.

'This expedition has to succeed,' the Chief said, and

his features blurred momentarily from sheer fatigue. 'In strictest confidence, there's considerable unrest on Grom. The Miner caste is on strike, for instance. They want a new digging shape. Say the old one is inefficient.'

Pid looked properly indignant. The Mining Shape had been set down by the Ancients fifty thousand years ago, together with the rest of the basic shapes. And now these upstarts wanted to change it!

'That's not all,' the Chief told him. 'We've uncovered a new Cult of Shapelessness. Picked up almost eight thousand Grom, and I don't know how many more we missed.'

Pid knew that Shapelessness was a lure of The Shapeless One, the greatest evil that the Grom mind could conceive of. But why, he wondered, did so many Grom fall for His lures?

The Chief guessed his question. 'Pid,' he said, 'I suppose it's difficult for you to understand. Do you enjoy Piloting?'

'Yes, sir,' Pid said simply. Enjoy Piloting! It was his entire life! Without a ship, he was nothing.

'Not all Grom feel that way,' the Chief said. 'I don't understand it either. All my ancestors have been Invasion Chiefs, back to the beginning of time. So of course *I* want to be an Invasion Chief. It's only natural, as well as lawful. But the lower castes don't feel that way.' The Chief shook his body sadly. 'I've told you this for a reason. We Grom need more room. This unrest is caused purely by crowding. All our psychologists say so. Another planet to expand into will cure everything. So we're counting on you, Pid.'

39

'Yes, sir,' Pid said, with a glow of pride.

The Chief rose to end the interview. Then he changed his mind and sat down again.

'You'll have to watch your crew,' he said. 'They're loyal, no doubt, but low-caste. And you know the lower castes.'

Pid did indeed.

'Ger your Detector is suspected of harbouring Alterationist tendencies. He was once fined for assuming a quasi-Hunter shape. Ilg has never had any definite charge brought against him. But I hear that he remains immobile for suspiciously long periods of time. Possibly, he fancies himself a Thinker.'

'But, sir,' Pid protested. 'If they are even slightly tainted with Alterationism or Shapelessness, why send them on this expedition?'

The Chief hesitated before answering. 'There are plenty of Grom I could trust,' he said slowly. 'But those two have certain qualities of resourcefulness and imagination that will be needed on this expedition.' He sighed. 'I really don't understand why those qualities are usually linked with Shapelessness.'

'Yes, sir,' Pid said.

'Just watch them.'

'Yes, sir,' Pid said again, and saluted, realizing that the interview was at an end. In his body pouch he felt the dormant Displacer ready to transform the enemy's power source into a bridge across space for the Grom hordes.

'Good luck,' the Chief said. 'I'm sure you'll need it.'

The ship dropped silently towards the surface of the enemy planet. Ger the Detector analysed the clouds below, and fed data into the Camouflage Unit. The Unit went to work. Soon the ship looked, to all outward appearances, like a cirrus formation.

Pid allowed the ship to drift slowly towards the surface of the mystery planet. He was in Optimum Pilot's Shape now, the most efficient of the four shapes allotted to the Pilot caste. Blind, deaf and dumb, an extension of his controls, all his attention was directed towards matching the velocities of the high-flying clouds, staying among them, becoming a part of them.

Ger remained rigidly in one of the two shapes allotted to Detectors. He fed data into the Camouflage Unit, and the descending ship slowly altered into an altocumulus.

There was no sign of activity from the enemy planet.

Ilg located an atomic power source, and fed the data to Pid. The Pilot altered course. He had reached the lowest level of clouds, barely a mile above the surface of the planet. Now his ship looked like a fat, fleecy cumulus.

And still there was no sign of alarm. The unknown fate that had overtaken twenty previous expeditions still had not showed itself.

Dusk crept across the face of the planet as Pid manoeuvred near the atomic power installation. He avoided the surrounding homes and hovered over a clump of woods.

Darkness fell, and the green planet's lone moon was veiled in clouds.

One cloud floated lower.

And landed.

'Quick, everyone out!' Pid shouted, detaching himself from the ship's controls. He assumed the Pilot's Shape best suited for running, and raced out the hatch.

Ger and Ilg hurried after him. They stopped fifty yards from the ship, and waited.

Inside the ship a little-used circuit closed. There was a silent shudder, and the ship began to melt. Plastic dissolved, metal crumpled. Soon the ship was a great pile of junk, and still the process went on. Big fragments broke into smaller fragments, and split, and split again.

Pid felt suddenly helpless, watching his ship scuttle itself. He was a Pilot, of the Pilot caste. His father had been a Pilot, and his father before him, stretching back to the hazy past when the Grom had first constructed ships. He had spent his entire childhood around ships, his entire manhood flying them.

Now, shipless, he was naked in an alien world.

In a few minutes there was only a mound of dust to show where the ship had been. The night wind scattered it through the forest. And then there was nothing at all.

They waited. Nothing happened. The wind sighed and the trees creaked. Squirrels chirped, and birds stirred in their nests. An acorn fell to the ground.

Pid heaved a sigh of relief and sat down. The twenty-first Grom expedition had landed safely.

There was nothing to be done until morning, so Pid began to make plans. They had landed as close to the atomic power installation as they dared. Now they would have to get closer. Somehow, one of them had to get very near the reactor room, in order to activate the Displacer.

Difficult, but Pid felt certain of success. After all, the Grom were strong on ingenuity.

Strong on ingenuity, he thought bitterly, but terribly

short of radioactives. That was another reason why this expedition was so important. There was little radioactive fuel left, on any of the Grom worlds. Ages ago, the Grom had spent their store of radioactives in spreading throughout their neighbouring worlds, occupying the ones that they could live on.

Now, colonization barely kept up with the mounting birthrate. New worlds were constantly needed.

This particular world, discovered in a scouting expedition, was needed. It suited the Grom perfectly. But it was too far away. They didn't have enough fuel to mount a conquering space fleet.

Luckily, there was another way. A better way.

Over the centuries, the Grom scientists had developed the Displacer. A triumph of Identity Engineering, the Displacer allowed mass to be moved instantaneously between any two linked points.

One end was set up at Grom's sole atomic energy plant. The other end had to be placed in proximity to another atomic power source, and activated. Diverted power then flowed through both ends, was modified, and modified again.

Then, through the miracle of Identity Engineering, the Grom could *step* through from planet to planet; or pour through in a great, overwhelming wave.

It was quite simple.

But twenty expeditions had failed to set up the Earth-end Displacer.

What had happened to them was not known.

For no Grom ship had ever returned to tell.

*

Before dawn they crept through the woods, taking on the colouration of the plants around them. Their Displacers pulsed feebly, sensing the nearness of atomic energy.

A tiny, four-legged creature darted in front of them. Instantly, Ger grew four legs and a long, streamlined body and gave chase.

'Ger! come back here!' Pid howled at the Detector, throwing caution to the winds.

Ger overtook the animal and knocked it down. He tried to bite it, but he had neglected to grow teeth. The animal jumped free, and vanished into the underbrush. Ger thrust out a set of teeth and bunched his muscles for another leap.

'*Ger!*'

Reluctantly, the Detector turned away. He loped silently back to Pid.

'I was hungry,' he said.

'You were not,' Pid said sternly.

'Was,' Ger mumbled, writhing with embarrassment.

Pid remembered what the Chief had told him. Ger certainly did have Hunter tendencies. He would have to watch him more closely.

'We'll have no more of that,' Pid said. 'Remember – the lure of Exotic Shapes is not sanctioned. Be content with the shape you were born to.'

Ger nodded and melted back into the underbrush. They moved on.

At the extreme edge of the woods they could observe the atomic energy installation. Pid disguised himself as a clump of shrubbery, and Ger formed himself into an old log. Ilg, after a moment's thought, became a young oak.

The installation was in the form of a long, low building, surrounded by a metal fence. There was a gate, and guards in front of it.

The first job, Pid thought, was to get past that gate. He began to consider ways and means.

From the fragmentary reports of the survey parties, Pid knew that, in some ways, this race of Men were like the Grom. They had pets, as the Grom did, and homes and children, and a culture. The inhabitants were skilled mechanically, as were the Grom.

But there were terrific differences, also. The Men were of fixed and immutable form, like stones or trees. And to compensate, their planet boasted a fantastic array of species, types and kinds. This was completely unlike Grom, which had only eight distinct forms of animal life.

And evidently, the Men were skilled at detecting invaders, Pid thought. He wished he knew how the other expeditions had failed. It would make his job much easier.

A man lurched past them on two incredibly stiff legs. Rigidity was evident in his every move. Without looking, he hurried past.

'I know,' Ger said, after the creature had moved away. 'I'll disguise myself as a Man, walk through the gate to the reactor room, and activate my Displacer.'

'You can't speak their language,' Pid pointed out.

'I won't speak at all. I'll ignore them. Look.' Quickly Ger shaped himself into a Man.

'That's not bad,' Pid said.

Ger tried a few practice steps, copying the bumpy walk of the Man.

'But I'm afraid it won't work,' Pid said.

'It's perfectly logical,' Ger pointed out.

'I know. Therefore the other expeditions must have tried it. And none of them came back.'

There was no arguing that. Ger flowed back into the shape of a log. 'What, then?' he asked.

'Let me think,' Pid asked.

Another creature lurched past, on four legs instead of two. Pid recognized it as a Dog, a pet of Man. He watched it carefully.

The Dog ambled to the gate, head down, in no particular hurry. It walked through, unchallenged, and lay down in the grass.

'H'm,' Pid said.

They watched. One of the Men walked past, and touched the Dog on the head. The Dog stuck out its tongue and rolled over on its side.

'I can do that,' Ger said excitedly. He started to flow into the shape of a Dog.

'No, wait,' Pid said. 'We'll spend the rest of the day thinking it over. This is too important to rush into.'

Ger subsided sulkily.

'Come on, let's move back,' Pid said. He and Ger started into the woods. Then he remembered Ilg.

'Ilg?' he called softly.

There was no answer.

'Ilg!'

'What? Oh, yes,' an oak tree said, and melted into a bush. 'Sorry. What were you saying?'

'We're moving back,' Pid said. 'Were you, by any chance, Thinking?'

'Oh, no,' Ilg assured him. 'Just resting.'

Pid let it go at that. There was too much else to worry about.

They discussed it for the rest of the day, hidden in the deepest part of the woods. The only alternatives seemed to be Man or Dog. A Tree couldn't walk past the gates, since that was not in the nature of trees. Nor could anything else, and escape notice.

Going as a Man seemed too risky. They decided that Ger would sally out in the morning as a Dog.

'Now get some sleep!' Pid said.

Obediently his two crewmen flattened out, going immediately Shapeless. But Pid had a more difficult time.

Everything looked too easy. Why wasn't the atomic installation better guarded? Certainly the Men must have learned something from the expeditions they had captured in the past. Or had they killed them without asking any questions?

You couldn't tell what an alien would do.

Was that open gate a trap?

Wearily he flowed into a comfortable position on the lumpy ground. Then he pulled himself together hastily.

He had gone Shapeless.

Comfort was not in the line of duty, he reminded himself, and firmly took a Pilot's Shape.

But a Pilot's Shape wasn't constructed for sleeping on damp, bumpy ground. Pid spent a restless night, thinking of ships, and wishing he were flying one.

He awoke in the morning tired and ill-tempered. He nudged Ger.

'Let's get this over with!' he said.

Ger flowed gaily to his feet.

'Come on, Ilg!' Pid said angrily, looking around. 'Wake up!'

There was no reply.

'Ilg!' he called.

Still there was no reply.

'Help me look for him!' Pid said to Ger. 'He must be around here somewhere.'

Together they tested every bush, tree, log and shrub in the vicinity. But none of them was Ilg.

Pid began to feel a cold panic run through him. What could have happened to the Radioman?

'Perhaps he decided to go through the gate on his own,' Ger suggested.

Pid considered the possibility. It seemed unlikely. Ilg had never shown much initiative. He had always been content to follow orders.

They waited. But midday came, and there was still no sign of Ilg.

'We can't wait any longer,' Pid said, and they started through the woods. Pid wondered if Ilg *had* tried to get through the gates on his own. Those quiet types often concealed a foolhardy streak.

But there was nothing to show that Ilg had been successful. He would have to assume that the Radioman was dead, or captured by the Men.

That left two of them to activate a Displacer.

And he still didn't know what had happened to the other expeditions.

At the edge of the woods, Ger turned himself into a facsimile of a Dog. Pid inspected him carefully.

'A little less tail,' he said.

Ger shortened his tail.

'More ears.'

Ger lengthened his ears.

'Now even them up.'

They became even.

Pid inspected the finished product. As far as he could tell, Ger was perfect, from the tip of his tail to his wet, black nose.

'Good luck!' Pid said.

'Thanks.' Cautiously Ger moved out of the woods, walking in the lurching style of Dogs and Men. At the gate the guard called to him. Pid held his breath.

Ger walked past the Man, ignoring him. The Man started to walk over. Ger broke into a run.

Pid shaped a pair of strong legs for himself, ready to dash if Ger was caught.

But the guard turned back to his gate. Ger stopped running immediately, and strolled quietly towards the main door of the building.

Pid dissolved his legs with a sigh of relief . . . and then tensed again.

The main door was closed.

Pid hoped the Radioman wouldn't try to open it. That was *not* in the nature of Dogs.

As he watched, another Dog came running towards Ger. Ger backed away from him. The Dog approached and sniffed. Ger sniffed back.

Then both of them ran around the building.

That was clever, Pid thought. There was bound to be a door in the rear.

He glanced up at the afternoon sun. As soon as the Displacer was activated, the Grom armies would begin to pour through. By the time the Men recovered from the shock, a million or more Grom troops would be here, weapons and all. With more following.

The day passed slowly, and nothing happened.

Nervously Pid watched the front of the plant. It shouldn't be taking so long, if Ger were successful.

Late into the night he waited. Men walked in and out of the installation, and Dogs barked around the gates. But Ger did not appear.

Ger had failed. Ilg was gone. Only he was left.

And *still* he didn't know what had happened.

By morning, Pid was in complete despair. He knew that the twenty-first Grom expedition to this planet was near the point of complete failure. Now it was all up to him.

He saw that workers were arriving in great number, rushing through the gates. He decided to take advantage of the apparent confusion, and started to shape himself into a Man.

A Dog walked past the woods where he was hiding.

'Hello,' the Dog said.

It was Ger.

'What happened?' Pid asked, with a sigh of relief. 'Why were you so long? Couldn't you get in?'

'I don't know,' Ger said, wagging his tail. 'I didn't try.'

Pid was speechless.

'I went hunting,' Ger said complacently. 'This form is ideal for Hunting, you know. I went out the rear gate with another Dog.'

'But the expedition – your duty—'

'I changed my mind,' Ger told him. 'You know, Pilot, I never wanted to be a Detector.'

'But you were *born* a Detector.'

'That's true,' Ger said. 'But it doesn't help. I always wanted to be a Hunter.'

Pid shook his entire body in annoyance. 'You can't,' he said, very slowly, as one would explain to a Gromling. 'The Hunter shape is forbidden to you.'

'Not here it isn't,' Ger said, still wagging his tail.

'Let's have no more of this!' Pid said angrily. 'Get into that installation and set up your Displacer! I'll try to over-look this heresy.'

'No,' Ger said. 'I don't want the Grom here. They'd ruin it for the rest of us.'

'He's right,' a nearby oak tree said.

'Ilg!' Pid gasped. 'Where are you?'

Branches stirred. 'I'm right here,' Ilg said. 'I've been Think-ing.'

'But – your caste—'

'Pilot,' Ger said sadly, 'why don't you wake up? Most of the people on Grom are miserable. Only custom makes us take the caste-shape of our ancestors.'

51

'Pilot,' Ilg said, 'all Grom are born Shapeless.'

'And being born Shapeless, all Grom should have Freedom of Shape,' Ger said.

'Exactly!' Ilg said. 'But he'll never understand. Now excuse me! I want to Think.' And the oak tree was silent.

Pid laughed humourlessly. 'The Men will kill you off,' he said. 'Just as they killed off all the other expeditions.'

'No one from Grom has been killed,' Ger told him. 'The other expeditions are right here.'

'Alive?'

'Certainly. The Men don't even know we exist. That Dog I was Hunting with is a Grom from the twelfth expedition. There are hundreds of us here, Pilot. We like it.'

Pid tried to absorb it all. He had always known that the lower castes were lax in caste-consciousness. But this was preposterous.

This planet's secret menace was – freedom.

'Join us, Pilot!' Ger said. 'We've got a paradise here. Do you know how many species there are on this Planet? An uncountable number! There's a shape to suit every need.'

Pid ignored them. Traitors!

He'd do the job all by himself.

So Men were unaware of the presence of the Grom. Getting near the reactor might not be so difficult after all. The others had failed in their duty because they were of the lower castes, weak and irresponsible. Even the Pilots among them must have been secretly sympathetic to the Cult of Shapelessness the Chief had mentioned, or the alien planet could never have swayed them.

What shape to assume for his attempt?

Pid considered.

A Dog might be best. Evidently Dogs could wander pretty much where they wished. If something went wrong, Pid could change his shape to meet the occasion.

'The Supreme Council will take care of all of you,' he snarled, and shaped himself into a small brown Dog. 'I'm going to set up the Displacer myself.'

He studied himself for a moment, bared his teeth at Ger, and loped towards the gate.

He loped for about ten feet and stopped in utter horror.

The smells rushed at him from all directions. Smells in a profusion and variety he had never dreamed existed. Smells that were harsh, sweet, sharp, heavy, mysterious, overpowering. Smells that terrified. Alien and repulsive and inescapable, the odours of Earth struck him like a blow.

He curled his lips and held his breath. He ran on for a few steps, and had to breathe again. He almost choked.

He tried to remould his Dog-nostrils to be less sensitive. It didn't work. It wouldn't, so long as he kept the Dog-shape. An attempt to modify his metabolism didn't work either.

All this in the space of two or three seconds. He was rooted in his tracks, fighting the smells, wondering what to do.

Then the noises hit him.

They were a constant and staggering roar, through which every tiniest whisper of sound stood out clearly and distinct. Sounds upon sounds – more noise than he had ever heard before at one time in his life. The woods behind him had suddenly become a madhouse.

Utterly confused, he lost control and became Shapeless.

He half-ran, half-flowed into a nearby bush. There he re-Shaped, obliterating the offending Dog ears and nostrils with vicious strokes of his thoughts.

The Dog-shape was out. Absolutely. Such appalling sharpness of senses might be fine for a Hunter such as Ger – he probably gloried in them. But another moment of such impressions would have driven Pid the Pilot mad.

What now? He lay in the bush and thought about it, while gradually his mind threw off the last effects of the dizzying sensory assault.

He looked at the gate. The Men standing there evidently hadn't noticed his fiasco. They were looking in another direction.

. . . a Man?

Well, it was worth a try.

Studying the Men at the gate, Pid carefully shaped himself into a facsimile – synthesis, actually, embodying one characteristic of that, another of this.

He emerged from the side of the bush opposite the gate, on his hands and knees. He sniffed the air, noting that the smells the Man-nostrils picked up weren't unpleasant at all. In fact, some of them were decidedly otherwise. It had just been the acuity of the Dog-nostrils, the number of smells they had detected and the near-brilliance with which they had done so, that had shocked him.

Also, the sounds weren't half so devastating. Only relatively close sounds stood out. All else was an undetailed whispering.

Evidently, Pid thought, it had been a long time since Men had been Hunters.

He tested his legs, standing up and taking a few clumsy steps. *Thud* of foot on ground. Drag the other leg forward in a heavy arc. *Thud*. Rocking from side to side, he marched back and forth behind the bush. His arms flapped as he sought balance. His head wobbled on its neck, until he remembered to hold it up. Head up, eyes down, he missed seeing a small rock. His heel turned on it. He sat down, hard.

The ankle hurt. Pid curled his Man-lips and crawled back into the bush.

The Man-shape was too unspeakably clumsy. It was offensive to plod one step at a time. Body held rigidly upright. Arms wobbling. There had been a deluge of sense-impressions in the Dog-shape; there was dull, stiff, half-alive inadequacy to the Man-shape.

Besides, it was dangerous, now that Pid thought it over, as well as distasteful. He couldn't control it properly. It wouldn't look right. Someone might question him. There was too much about Men he didn't – couldn't – know. The planting of the Displacer was too important a thing for him to fumble again. Only luck had kept him from being seen during the sensory onslaught.

The Displacer in his body pouch pulsed and tugged, urging him to be on his way towards the distant reactor room.

Grimly, Pid let out the last breath he had taken with his Man-lungs, and dissolved the lungs.

What shape to take?

Again he studied the gate, the Men standing beside it,

the building beyond in which was the all-important reactor.

A small shape was needed. A fast one. An unobtrusive one.

He lay and thought.

The bush rustled above him. A small brown shape had fluttered down to light on a twig. It hopped to another twig, twittering. Then it fluttered off in a flash, and was gone.

That, Pid thought, was it.

A Sparrow that was not a Sparrow rose from the bush a few moments later. An observer would have seen it circle the bush, diving, hedgehopping, even looping, as if practising all manoeuvres possible to Sparrows.

Pid tensed his shoulder muscles, inclined his wings. He slipped off to the right, approached the bush at what seemed breakneck speed, though he knew this was only because of his small size. At the last second he lifted his tail. Not quite quickly enough. He swooped up and over the top of the bush, but his legs brushed the top leaves, his beak went down, and he stumbled in air for a few feet back-forward.

He blinked beady eyes as if at a challenge. Back towards the bush at a fine clip, again up and over. This time cleanly.

He chose a tree. Zoomed into its network of branches, wove a web of flight, working his way around and around the trunk, over and under branches that flashed before him, through crotches with no more than a feather's breadth to spare.

At last he rested on a low branch, and found himself chirping in delight.

The tree extruded a feeler from the branch he sat on, and touched his wings and tail.

'Interesting,' said the tree. 'I'll have to try that shape some time.'

Ilg.

'Traitor,' hissed Pid, growing a mouth in his chest to hiss it, and then he did something that caused Ilg to exclaim in outrage.

Pid flew out of the woods. Over the underbrush and across the open space towards the gate.

This body would do the trick!

This body would do anything!

He rose, in a matter of a few Sparrow heartbeats, to an altitude of a hundred feet. From here the gate, the Men, the building were small, sharp shapes against a green-brown mat. Pid found that he could see not only with unaccustomed clarity, but with a range of vision that astonished him. To right and to left he could see far into the hazy blue of the sky, and the higher he rose the farther he could see.

He rose higher.

The Displacer pulsed, reminding him of the job he had to do.

He stiffened his wings and glided, regretfully putting aside his desires to experiment with this wonderful shape, at least for the present. After he planted the Displacer, he would go off by himself for a while and do it just a little more – somewhere where Ilg and Ger would not see him – before the Grom Army arrived and the invasion began.

He felt a tiny twinge of guilt, as he circled. It was Evil to want to keep this alien flying shape any longer than was absolutely necessary to the performance of his duty. It was a device of the Shapeless One. . . .

But what had Ilg said? *All Grom are born Shapeless.* It was true. Grom children were amorphous, until old enough to be instructed in the caste-shape of their ancestors.

Maybe it wasn't *too* great a sin to alter your Shape, then – just once in a long while. After all, one must be fully aware of the nature of Evil in order to meaningfully reject it.

He had fallen lower in circling. The Displacer pulse had strengthened. For some reason it irritated him. He drove higher on strong wings, circled again. Air rushed past him – a smooth, whispering flow, pierced by his beak, streaming invisibly past his sharp eyes, moving along his body in tiny turbulences that moved his feathers against his skin.

It occurred to him – or rather struck him with considerable force – that he was satisfying a longing of his Pilot Caste that went far deeper than Piloting.

He drove powerfully with his wings, felt tonus across his back, shot forward and up. He thought of the controls of his ship. He imagined flowing into them, becoming part of them, as he had so often done – and for the first time in his life the thought failed to excite him.

No machine could compare with this!

What he would give to have wings of his own!

. . . *Get from my sight, Shapeless One!*

The Displacer must be planted, activated. All Grom depended on him.

He eyed the building, far below. He would pass over it. The Displacer would tell him which window to enter – which window was so near the reactor that he could do his job before the Men even knew he was about.

He started to drop lower, and the Hawk struck.

It had been above him. His first inkling of danger was the sharp pain of talons in his back, and the stunning blow of a beak across his head.

Dazed, he let his back go Shapeless. His body-substance flowed from the grasp of the talons. He dropped a dozen feet and resumed Sparrow-shape, hearing an astonished squawk from the attacker.

He banked, and looked up. The Hawk was eyeing him.

Talons spread again. The sharp beak gaped. The Hawk swooped.

Pid had to fight as a Bird, naturally. He was four hundred feet above the ground.

So he became an impossibly deadly Bird.

He grew to twice the size of the Hawk. He grew a foot-long beak with a double razor's edge. He grew talons like six-inch scimitars. His eyes gleamed a red challenge.

The Hawk broke flight, squalling in alarm. Frantically, tail down and widespread, it thundered its wings and came to a dead stop six feet from Pid.

Looking thoughtfully at Pid, it allowed itself to plummet. It fell a hundred feet, spread its wings, stretched its neck and flew off so hastily that its wings became blurs.

Pid saw no reason to pursue it.

Then, after a moment, he did.

He glided, keeping the Hawk in sight, thoughts racing, feeling the newness, the power, the wonder of Freedom of Shape.

Freedom . . .

He did not want to give it up.

The bird-shape was wondrous. He would experiment with it. Later, he might tire of it for a time and assume another – a crawling or running shape, or even a swimming one. The possibilities for excitement, for adventure, for fulfilment and simple sensual pleasure were endless!

Freedom of Shape was – obviously, now that you thought on it – the Grom birthright. And the caste-system was artificial – obviously. A device for political and priestly benefit – obviously.

Go away, Shapeless One . . . this does not concern you.

He rose to a thousand feet, two thousand, three. The Displacer's pulse grew feebler and finally vanished.

At four thousand feet he released it and watched it spin downward, vanish into a cloud.

Then he set out after the Hawk, which was now only a dot on the horizon. He would find out how the Hawk had broken flight as it had – skidded on air – he wanted to do that too! There were so many things he wanted to learn about flying. In a week, he thought, he should be able to duplicate all the skill that millennia had evolved into Birds. Then his new life would really begin.

He became a torpedo-shape with huge wings, and sped after the Hawk.

The Impacted Man

TO: CENTRE
   Office 41
ATTN: Controller Miglese
FROM: Contractor Carienomen
SUBJ: ATTALA Metagalaxy

Dear Controller Miglese:

This is to inform you that I have completed contract 13371A. In the region of space coded ATTALA I have constructed one metagalaxy, incorporating 549 billion galaxies, with the normal distribution of star clusters, variables, novae, et cetera. See attached data sheet.

The outer limits of ATTALA metagalaxy are defined in the accompanying map.

Speaking for myself, as chief designer, and for my company, I am confident that we have done a sound construction job, as well as a work of great artistic merit.

We welcome your inspection.

Having fulfilled the terms of our contract, the agreed-upon fee is payable at any time.

Respectfully,
Carienomen

Enclosed:
1 data sheet, installations
1 map of metagalaxy ATTALA

TO: Construction Headquarters
   334132, Extension 12
ATTN: Chief Designer, Carienomen
FROM: Asst. Controller Miglese
SUBJ: ATTALA Metagalaxy

Dear Carienomen:

We have inspected your construction, and have held up your fee accordingly. Artistic? I suppose it's artistic. But haven't you forgotten our prime concern in construction work?

   Consistency, just to remind you.

   Our inspectors discovered large amounts of unexplained data occurring even around the meta-galactic centre, a region one would think you would build with care. That can't go on. Luckily, the region is unpopulated.

   And that's not all. Would you care to explain your spatial phenomena? What in chaos is this red shift you've built in? I've read your explanation of it, and it doesn't make any sense to me. How will planetary observers take it?

   Artistry is no excuse.

   Furthermore, what kinds of atoms are you using? Carienomen, are you trying to save money with shoddy materials? A good percentage of those atoms

*were unstable. They break down at the touch of a
finger or even without the touch of a finger. Couldn't
you figure out any other way of lighting your suns?*

*Enclosed is a data sheet, outlining the findings of
our inspectors. No payment until they're cleared up.*

*And there is another serious matter, just brought
to my attention. Evidently you weren't watching too
closely for stresses and strains in your spatial fabric.
We have detected a time-flaw near the periphery of one
of your galaxies. It is small, at present, but it could
grow. I suggest that you take care of it at once, before
you have to rebuild a galaxy or two.*

*One of the inhabitants of a planet impinging on the
flaw is impacted already; wedged into the flaw, due
entirely to your carelessness. I suggest that you correct
this before he moves out of his normal time-sequence,
creating paradoxes right and left.*

Get in touch with him, if need be!

*Also, I have word of unexplained phenomena on
some of your planets; items such as flying pigs, moving
mountains, ghosts, and others, all enumerated in the
complaint sheet.*

*We won't have this sort of thing, Carienomen! A
paradox is strictly forbidden in the created galaxies,
since a paradox is the inevitable forerunner of chaos.*

*Take care of that impaction at once. I don't know
whether the impacted individual realizes it yet.*

Miglese

Enclosed:
1 complaint sheet

Kay Masrin folded the last blouse into the suitcase, and, with her husband's assistance, closed it.

'That's that,' Jack Masrin said, hefting the bulging case. 'Say good-bye to the old homestead.' They looked around at the furnished room where they had spent their last year.

'Good-bye, homestead,' Kay said. 'Let's not miss the train.'

'Plenty of time.' Masrin started to the door. 'Shall we say good-bye to Happy Boy?' They had given Mr Harf, their landlord, that nickname because he smiled, once a month, when they handed him the rent. Of course, he immediately reshaped his mouth to its usual prim line.

'Let's not,' Kay said, smoothing out her tailored suit. 'He just might wish us luck, and what would happen then?'

'You're perfectly right,' Masrin said. 'No use starting a new life with Happy Boy's blessings. I'd rather have the Witch of Endor curse me.'

With Kay following him, Masrin walked to the head of the stairs. He looked down at the first-floor landing, started to take the first step, and stopped abruptly.

'What's wrong?' Kay asked.

'Have we forgotten anything?' Masrin asked, frowning.

'I checked all the drawers and under the bed. Come on, we'll be late.'

Masrin looked down the stairs again. Something was bothering him. He searched quickly for the source of the trouble. Of course, they had practically no money. But that had never worried him in the past. He *did* have a teaching job, finally, even if it was in Iowa. That was the important thing, after a year of working in a bookstore. Everything was going right. Why should he be worried?

He took a step down, and stopped again. The feeling was stronger. There was something he shouldn't do. He glanced back at Kay.

'Do you hate leaving that much?' Kay asked. 'Let's go, or Happy Boy'll charge us another month's rent. Which, for some strange reason, we haven't got.'

Still Masrin hesitated. Kay pushed past him and trotted downstairs.

'See?' she said from the first-floor landing. 'It's easy. Come on. Walk to Mummy.'

Masrin mumbled a few subdued curses and started down the stairs. The feeling became stronger.

He reached the eighth step, and—

He was standing on a grassy plain. The transition was as sudden as that.

He gasped and blinked. The suitcase was still in his hand. But where was the brownstone? Where was Kay? Where, for that matter, was New York?

In the distance was a small blue mountain. There was a clump of trees nearby. In front of the clump was a dozen or so men.

Masrin was in a dreamlike state of shock. He observed, almost idly, that the men were short, swarthy, thickly muscled. They wore loin cloths, and carried beautifully carved and polished clubs.

They were watching him, and Masrin decided it was a toss-up, who was the most surprised.

Then one of them grunted something, and they started moving towards him.

A club bounced off his suitcase.

The shock dissolved. Masrin turned, dropped the suitcase and ran like a greyhound. A club whacked his spine, nearly knocking him over. He was facing a little hill, and he bounded up it, arrows showering around him.

A few feet up, he realised that he was back in New York.

He was at the top of the stairs, still in full stride, and before he could stop himself he had run into the wall. Kay was on the first-floor landing, looking up. She gasped when she saw him, but didn't say anything.

Masrin looked at the familiar murky mauve walls of the brownstone, and at his wife.

No savages.

'What happened?' Kay whispered, white-faced, coming up the stairs.

'What did you see?' Masrin asked. He didn't have a chance to see the full impact of what had happened. Ideas were pouring into his head, theories, conclusions.

Kay hesitated, gnawing at her lower lip. 'You walked down a couple of steps and then you were gone. I couldn't see you any more. I just stood there and looked and looked. And then I heard a noise, and you were back on the stairs. Running.'

They walked back to their room and opened the door. Kay sat down at once on the bed. Masrin walked around, catching his breath. Ideas were still pouring in, and he was having trouble sifting them.

'You won't believe me,' he said.

'Oh won't I? Try me!'

He told her about the savages.

'You could tell me you were on Mars,' Kay said. 'I'd believe you. I saw you disappear.'

'My suitcase!' Masrin said suddenly, remembering that he had dropped it.

'Forget the suitcase,' Kay said.

'I have to go back for it,' Masrin said.

'No!'

'I must. Look, dear, it's pretty obvious what happened. I walked through some sort of time-flaw, which sent me back to the past. I must have landed in prehistoric times, to judge by the welcoming committee I met. I have to go back for that suitcase.'

'Why?' Kay asked.

'Because I can't allow a paradox to occur.' Masrin didn't even wonder how he knew this. His normal egotism saved him from wondering how the idea had originated in his mind.

'Look,' he said, 'my suitcase lands in the past. In it I've got an electric shaver, some pants with zippers, a plastic hairbrush, a nylon shirt, and a dozen or so books – some of them published as late as 1951. I've even got Ettison's *Western Ways* in there, a text on Western civilization from 1490 to the present day.

'The contents of that case could give these savages the impetus to change their own history. And suppose some of that got into the hands of Europeans, after they discovered America? How would that affect the present.

'I don't know,' Kay said. 'And you don't either.'

'Of course I know,' Masrin said. It was all crystal-clear. He was amazed that she wasn't able to follow it

'Look at it this way,' Masrin said. 'Minutiae makes history. The present is made up of a tremendous number of infinitesimal factors, which shaped and moulded the past. If you add another factor to the past, you're bound to get another result in the present. But the present is as it is, unchangeable. So we have a paradox. And there can't be any paradox.'

'Why can't there?' Kay asked.

Masrin frowned. For a bright girl, she was following him very poorly. 'Just believe me,' he said. 'Paradox isn't allowed in a logical universe.' Allowed by whom? He had the answer.

'The way I see it,' Masrin said, 'there must be a regulating principle in the universe. All our natural laws are expressions of it. This principle can't stand paradox, because – because—' He knew that the answer had to do with suppressing the fundamental chaos, but he didn't know why.

'Anyhow, this principle can't stand paradox.'

'Where did you get that idea?' Kay asked. She had never heard Jack talk that way before.

'I've had these ideas for a long time,' Masrin said, and believed it. 'There was just never any reason to talk about it. Anyhow, I'm going back for my suitcase.'

He walked out to the landing, followed by Kay. 'Sorry I can't bring you any souvenirs,' Masrin said cheerfully. 'Unfortunately, that would result in a paradox also. Everything in the past has had a part in shaping the present. Remove something, and it's like removing one unknown from an equation. You wouldn't get the same result.' He started down the stairs.

On the eighth step, he disappeared again.

He was back in prehistoric America. The savages were gathered around the suitcase, only a few feet from him. They hadn't opened it yet, Masrin noticed thankfully. Of course, the suitcase itself was a pretty paradoxical article. But its appearance – and his – would probably be swallowed up in myth and legend. Time had a certain amount of flexibility.

Looking at them, Masrin couldn't decide if they were forerunners of Indians, or a separate sub-race which didn't survive. He wondered if they thought he was an enemy, or a garden-variety evil spirit.

Masrin darted forward, shoved two of them aside, and grabbed his suitcase. He ran back, circling the little hill, and stopped.

He was still in the past.

Where in chaos was that hole in time, Masrin wondered, not noticing the strangeness of his oath. The savages were coming after him now, starting around the little hill. Masrin almost had the answer, then lost it as an arrow sped past him. He sprinted, trying to keep the hill between himself and the Indians. His long legs pumped, and a club bounced behind him.

Where was that hole in time? What if it had moved? Perspiration poured from his face as he ran. A club grazed his arm, and he twisted around the side of the hill, looking wildly for shelter.

He met three squat savages, coming after him.

Masrin fell to the ground as they swung their clubs, and they tripped over his body. Others were coming now, and he jumped to his feet.

Up! The thought struck him suddenly, cutting through his fear. Up!

He charged the hill, certain that he would never reach the top alive.

And he was back in the boarding house, still holding the suitcase.

'Are you hurt, darling?' Kay put her arms around him. 'What happened?'

Masrin had only one rational thought. He couldn't remember any prehistoric tribe that carved their clubs as elaborately as these savages. It was almost a unique art form, and he wished he could get one of the clubs to a museum.

Then he looked at the mauve walls wildly, expecting to see the savages come bounding out of them. Or perhaps there were little men in his suitcase. He fought for control. The thinking portion of his mind told him not to be alarmed; flaws in time were possible, and he had become wedged, impacted in one. Everything else followed logically. All he had to do—

But another part of his mind wasn't interested in logic. It had been staring blankly at the impossibility of the whole thing, uninfluenced by any rational arguments. That part knew an impossibility when it saw one, and said so.

Masrin screamed and fainted.

TO: *CENTRE*
 Office 41
ATTN: *Asst. Controller Miglese*
FROM: *Contractor Carienomen*
SUBJ: *ATTALA Metagalaxy*

Dear Sir:

I consider your attitude unfair. True, I have utilized some new ideas in my approach to this particular metagalaxy. I have allowed myself the latitude of artistry, never thinking I would be beset by the howls of a static, reactionary CENTRE.

Believe me, I am as interested as you in our great job – that of suppressing the fundamental chaos. But in doing this, we must not sacrifice our values.

Enclosed is a statement of defence concerning my use of the red shift, and another statement of the advantages gained by using a small percentage of unstable atoms for lighting and energy purposes.

As to the time-flaw, that was merely a small error in duration-flow, and has nothing to do with the fabric of space, which is, I assure you, of first-rate quality.

There is, as you pointed out, an individual impacted in the flaw, which makes the job of repair slightly more difficult. I have been in contact with him, indirectly, of course, and have succeeded in giving him a limited understanding of his role.

If he doesn't disturb the flaw too much by time-travelling, I should be able to sew it up with little difficulty. I don't know if this procedure is possible, though. My rapport with him is quite shaky, and he seems to have a number of strong influences around him, counselling him to move.

I could perform an extraction of course, and ultimately I may have to do just that. For that matter, if the thing gets out of hand I may be forced to extract the entire planet. I hope not, since that would necessitate clearing that entire portion of space, where there are also local observers. This, in turn, might necessitate rebuilding an entire galaxy.

However, I hope to have the problem settled by the time I next communicate with you.

The warp in the metagalactic centre was caused by some workmen leaving a disposal unit open. It has been closed.

The phenomena such as walking mountains, et cetera, are being handled in the usual way. Payment is still due on my work.

Respectfully,
Carienomen

Enclosed:
1 statement, 5541 pages, Red Shift
1 statement, 7689 pages, Unstable Atoms

TO: Construction Headquarters
334132, Extension 12
ATTN: Contractor Carienomen
FROM: Asst. Controller Miglese
SUBJ: ATTALA Metagalaxy

Carienomen:

You will be paid after you can show me a logical, decently constructed job. I'll read your statements when and if I have time. Take care of the flaw-impaction before it tears a hole in the fabric of space!

Miglese

Masrin recovered his nerve in half an hour. Kay put a compress on a purple bruise on his arm. Masrin started pacing the room. Once again, he was in complete possession of his faculties. Ideas started to come.

'The past is down,' he said, half to Kay, half to himself. 'I don't mean really "down"; but when I move in that apparent direction, I step through the hole in time. It's a case of shifted conjoined dimensionality.'

'What does that mean?' Kay asked, staring wide-eyed at her husband.

'Just take my word for it,' Masrin said, 'I can't go down!' He couldn't explain it to her any better. There weren't words to fit the concepts.

'Can you go up?' Kay asked, completely confused.

'I don't know. I suppose, if I went up, I'd go into the future.'

'Oh, I can't stand it,' Kay said. 'What's wrong with you? How will you get out of here? How will you get down that haunted staircase?'

'Are you people still there?' Mr Harf's voice croaked from outside. Masrin walked over and opened the door.

'I think we're going to stay for a while,' he said to the landlord.

73

'You're not,' Harf said. 'I've already rented this room again.' Happy Boy Harf was small and bony, with a narrow skull and lips as thin as a spider's thread. He stalked into the room, looking around for signs of damage to his property. One of Mr Harf's little idiosyncrasies was his belief that the nicest people were capable of the worst crimes.

'When are the people coming?' Masrin asked.

'This afternoon. And I want you out before they get here.'

'Couldn't we make some arrangement?' Masrin asked. The impossibility of the situation struck him. He couldn't go downstairs. If Harf forced him out, he would have to go to prehistoric New York, where he was sure his return was eagerly awaited.

And there was the over-all problem of paradox.

'I'm sick,' Kay said in a stifled little voice. 'I can't leave yet.'

'What are you sick from? I'll call an ambulance if you're sick,' Harf said, looking suspiciously around the room for any signs of bubonic plague.

'I'd gladly pay you double the rent if you'd let us stay a little longer,' Masrin said.

Harf scratched his head, and stared at Masrin. He wiped his nose on the back of his hand, and said, 'Where's the money?'

Masrin realized that he had about ten dollars left, and his train tickets. He and Kay were going to ask for an advance as soon as they reached the college.

'Broke,' Harf said. 'I thought you had a job at some school?'

'He does,' Kay said staunchly.

'Then why don't you go there and get out of my place?' Harf asked.

The Masrins were silent. Harf glared at them.

'Very suspicious. Get out before noon, or I'll call a cop!'

'Hold it!' Masrin said. 'We've paid the rent for today. The room's ours until twelve midnight.'

Harf stared at them. He wiped his nose again, thoughtfully.

'Don't try staying one minute over,' he said, stamping out of the room.

As soon as Harf was gone, Kay hurried over and closed the door. 'Honey,' she said, 'why don't you call up some scientists here in New York and tell them what's happened? I am sure they'd arrange something, until – how long will we have to stay here?'

'Until the flaw's repaired,' Masrin said. 'But we can't tell anyone; especially, we can't tell any scientists.'

'Why not?' Kay asked.

'Look, the important thing, as I told you, is to avoid a paradox. That means I have to keep my hands off the past, and the future. Right?'

'If you say so,' Kay said.

'We call in a team of scientists, and what happens? Naturally, they're sceptical. They want to *see* me do it. So I do it. Immediately, they bring in a few of their colleagues. *They* watch me disappear. Understand, all this time there's no proof that I've gone into the past. All they know is, if I walk downstairs, I disappear.

75

'Photographers are called in, to make sure I'm not hypnotizing the scientists. Then they demand proof. They want me to bring back a scalp, or one of those carved clubs. The newspapers get hold of it. It's inevitable that somewhere along the line I produce a paradox. And do you know what happens then?'

'No, and you don't either.'

'I do,' Masrin said firmly. 'Once a paradox is caused, the agent – the man who caused it – me – disappears. For good. And it goes down in the books as another unsolved mystery. That way, the paradox is resolved in its easiest way – by getting rid of the paradoxical element.'

'If you think you're in danger, then of course we won't call in any scientists,' Kay said. 'Although I wish I knew what you were driving at. I don't understand anything you've said.' She went to the window and looked out. There was New York, and beyond it, somewhere, was Iowa, where they should be going. She looked at her watch. They had already missed the train.

'Phone the college,' Masrin said. 'Tell them I'll be delayed a few days.'

'Will it be a few days?' Kay asked. 'How will you ever get out?'

'Oh, the hole in time isn't permanent,' Masrin said confidently. 'It'll heal – if I don't go sticking myself in it.'

'But we can only stay here until midnight. What happens then?'

'I don't know,' Masrin said. 'We can only hope it'll be fixed by then.'

TO: CENTRE
   Office 41
ATTN: Asst. Controller Miglese
FROM: Contractor Carienomen
SUBJ: MORSTT Metagalaxy

   Dear Sir:

   *Herein, enclosed, is my bid for work on the new
metagalaxy in the region coded MORSTT. If you have
heard any discussions in art circles recently, I think that
you will see that my use of unstable atoms in ATTALA
Metagalaxy has been proclaimed 'the first great
advance in creative engineering since the invention of
variable time-flow'. See the enclosed reviews.*
   My artistry has stirred many favourable comments.
   *Most of the inconsistencies – natural inconsistencies,
let me remind you – in ATTALA Metagalaxy have been
corrected. I am still working with the man impacted in
the time flow. He is proving quite co-operative; at least,
as co-operative as he can be, with the various influences
around him.*
   *To date, I have coalesced the edges of the flaw, and
am allowing them to harden. I hope the individual
remains immobile, since I really don't like to extract
anyone or anything. After all, each person, each
planet, each star system, no matter how minute, has
an integral part in my metagalactic scheme.*
   Artistically, at any rate.
   *Your inspection is welcomed again. Please note
the galactic configurations around the metagalactic*

centre. They are a dream of beauty you will wish to carry with you always.

Please consider my bid for the MORSTT Metagalaxy project in light of my past achievements.

Payment is still due on ATTALA Metagalaxy.

Respectfully,
Carienomen

Enclosed:
1 bid, for MORSTT Metagalaxy project
3 critical reviews, ATTALA Metagalaxy

'It's eleven forty-five, honey,' Kay said nervously. 'Do you think we could go now?'

'Let's wait a few minutes longer,' Masrin said. He could hear Harf prowling around on the landing, waiting eagerly for the dot of twelve.

Masrin watched the seconds tick by on his watch.

At five minutes to twelve, he decided that he might as well find out. If the hole wasn't fixed by now, another five minutes wouldn't do it.

He placed the suitcase on the dresser, and moved a chair next to it.

'What are you doing?' Kay asked.

'I don't feel like trying those stairs at night,' Masrin said. 'It's bad enough playing with those pre-Indians in the daylight. I'm going to try going up, instead.' His wife gave him an under-the-eyelids now-I-know-you're-cracking look.

'It's not the stairs that does it,' Masrin told her again. 'It's the act of going up or down. The critical distance seems to be about five feet. This will do just as well.'

Kay stood nervously, clenching and unclenching both hands, as Masrin climbed on the chair and put one foot on the dresser. Then the other, and he stood up.

'I think it's all right,' he said, teetering a little. 'I'm going to try it a little higher.'

He climbed on the suitcase.

And disappeared.

It was day, and he was in a city. But the city didn't look like New York. It was breathtakingly beautiful – so beautiful that Masrin didn't dare breathe, for fear of disturbing its fragile loveliness.

It was a place of delicate, wispy towers and buildings. And people. But what people, Masrin thought, letting out his breath with a sigh.

The people were blue-skinned. The light was green, coming from a green-tinged sun.

Masrin drew in a breath of air, and strangled. He gasped again, and started to lose his balance. There was no air in the place! At least, no air he could breathe. He felt for a step behind him, and then tumbled down—

To land, choking and writhing, on the floor of his room.

After a few moments he could breathe again. He heard Harf pounding on the door. Masrin staggered to his feet, and tried to think of something. He knew Harf; the man was probably certain by now that Masrin headed the Mafia. He would call a cop if they didn't leave. And that would ultimately result in—

'Listen,' he said to Kay, 'I've got another idea.' His

throat was burning from the atmosphere of the future. However, he told himself, there was no reason why he should be surprised. He had made quite a jump forward. The composition of the Earth's atmosphere must have changed, gradually, and the people had adapted to it. But it was a poison for him.

'There are two possibilities now,' he said to Kay. 'One, that under the prehistoric layer is another, earlier layer. Two, that the prehistoric layer is only a temporary discontinuity. That under it, is present New York again. Follow me?'

'No.'

'I'm going to try going under the prehistoric layer. It might get me down to the ground floor. Certainly, it can't be any worse.' Kay considered the logic of going some thousands of years into the past in order to walk ten feet, but didn't say anything.

Masrin opened the door and went out to the stairs, followed by Kay. 'Wish me luck!' he said.

'Luck, nothing,' Mr Harf said, on the landing. 'Just get out of here!'

Masrin plunged down the stairs.

It was still morning in prehistoric New York, and the savages were still waiting for him. Masrin estimated that only about half an hour had gone by here. He didn't have time to wonder why.

He had caught them by surprise, and was twenty yards away before they saw him. They followed, and Masrin looked for a depression. He had to go down five feet, in order to get out.

He found a shelving of the land, and jumped down.

He was in water. Not just on the surface, but *under*. The pressure was tremendous, and Masrin could not see sunlight above him.

He must have gone through to a time when this section was under the Atlantic.

Masrin kicked furiously, eardrums bursting. He started to rise towards the surface, and—

He was back on the plain, dripping wet.

This time, the savages had had enough. They looked at him, materialized in front of them, gave a shriek of horror, and bolted.

This water sprite was too strong for them.

Wearily, Masrin walked back to the hill, climbed it, and was back in the brownstone.

Kay was staring at him, and Harf's jaw was hanging slack. Masrin grinned weakly.

'Mr Harf,' he said, 'will you come into my room? There's something I want to tell you.'

TO: CENTRE
    Office 41
ATTN: *Asst. Controller Miglese*
FROM: *Contractor Carienomen*
SUBJ: *MORSTT Metagalaxy*

My Dear Sir:

I cannot understand your reply to my bid for the job of constructing MORSTT Metagalaxy. Moreover, I do not think that obscenity has any place in a business letter.

If you have taken the trouble to inspect my latest work in ATTALA, you will see that it is, take it all for all, a beautiful job, and one that will go a long way towards holding back the fundamental chaos.

The only detail left to attend to is the matter of the impacted man. I fear I shall have to extract.

The flaw was hardening nicely, when he blundered into it again, tearing it worse than ever. No paradox as yet, but I can see one coming.

Unless he can control his immediate environment, and do it at once, I shall take the necessary step. Paradox is not allowed.

I consider it my duty to ask you to reconsider my bid for the MORSTT Metagalaxy project.

And I trust you will excuse me for bringing this oversight to your attention, but payment is still due.

> *Respectfully,*
> *Carienomen*

'So that's the story, Mr Harf,' Masrin said, an hour later. 'I know how weird it sounds; but you saw me disappear yourself.'

'That I did,' Harf said. Masrin went into the bathroom to hang up his wet clothes.

'Yes,' Harf said, 'I guess you disappeared at that.'

'I certainly did.'

'And you don't want the scientists to know about your deal with the devil?' Harf asked slyly.

'No! I explained about paradox and—'

'Let me see!' Harf said. He wiped his nose vigorously.

'Those carved clubs you said they had. Wouldn't one of those be valuable to a museum? You said there was nothing like it.'

'What?' Masrin asked, coming out of the bathroom. 'Listen, I can't touch any of that stuff. It'll result in—'

'Of course,' Harf said, 'I could call in some newspaper boys instead. And some scientists. I could probably make me a nice pile out of this devil-worship.'

You wouldn't,' Kay said, remembering only that her husband had said something bad would happen.

'Be reasonable!' Harf said. 'All I want is one or two of those clubs. That won't cause any trouble. You can just ask your devil—'

'There's no devil involved,' Masrin said. 'You have no idea what part one of those clubs might have played in history. The club I take might have killed the man who would have united these people, and the North American Indians might have met the Europeans as a single nation. Think how that would change—'

'Don't hand me that stuff,' Harf said. 'Are you getting me a club or aren't you?'

'I've explained it to you,' Masrin said wearily.

'And don't tell me any more about this paradox business. I don't understand it, anyhow. But I'll split fifty-fifty with you on what I get for the club.'

'No.'

'O.K. I'll be seeing you.' Harf started for the door.

'Wait!'

'Yes?' Harf's thin, spidery mouth was smiling now.

Masrin examined his choice of evils. If he brought back a club there was a good chance of starting a paradox, by removing all that the club had done in the past. But if he didn't, Harf would call in the newspapers and scientists. They could find out if Harf was speaking the truth by simply carrying him downstairs; something the police would do anyhow. He would disappear, and then—

With more people in on it, a paradox would be inevitable. And all Earth might, very possibly, be removed. Although he didn't know why, Masrin knew this for a certainty.

He was lost either way, but getting the club seemed the simpler alternative.

'I'll get it,' Masrin said. He walked to the staircase, followed by Kay and Harf. Kay grabbed his hand.

'Don't do it!' she said.

'There's nothing else I can do.' He thought for a moment of killing Harf. But that would only result in the electric chair for him. Of course, he could kill Harf and take his body into the past, and bury it.

But the corpse of a twentieth-century man in prehistoric America might constitute a paradox, anyhow. Suppose it was dug up?

Besides, he didn't have it in him to kill a man.

Masrin kissed his wife, and walked downstairs.

There were no savages in sight on the plain, although Masrin thought he could feel their eyes, watching him. He found two clubs on the ground. The ones that struck him must be taboo, he decided, and picked one up, expecting another to crush his skull any moment. But the plain was silent.

'Good boy!' Harf said. 'Hand it here!' Masrin handed him the club. He went over to Kay and put his arm around her. It was a paradox now, as certainly as if he had killed his great-great-grandfather before he was born. 'That's a lovely thing,' Harf said, admiring the club under the light. 'Consider your rent paid for the rest of the month—'

The club disappeared from his hand.

Harf disappeared.

Kay fainted.

Masrin carried her to the bed, and splashed water on her face.

'What happened?' she asked.

'I don't know,' Masrin said, suddenly very puzzled about everything. 'All I know is, we're going to stay here for at least two weeks. Even if we have to eat beans.'

TO: CENTRE
   Office 41
ATTN: Asst. Controller Miglese
FROM: Contractor Carienomen
SUBJ: MORSTT Metagalaxy

Sir:

Your offer of a job repairing damaged stars is an insult to my company and myself. We refuse. Let me point out my work in the past, outlined in the brochure I am enclosing. How can you offer so menial a job to one of CENTRE'S greatest companies?

Again, I would like to put in my request for work on the new MORSTT Metagalaxy.

As for ATTALA Metagalaxy – the work is now completed, and a finer job cannot be found anywhere this side of chaos. The place is a wonder.

The impacted man is no longer impacted. I was forced to extract. However, I did not extract the man himself. Instead, I was able to remove one of the external influences on him. Now he can grow out normally.

A nice job, I think you'll admit, and solved with the ingenuity that characterizes all my work.

My decision was: Why extract a good man, when I could save him by pulling the rotten one beside him?

Again, I welcome your inspection. I request reconsideration on MORSTT Metagalaxy.
PAYMENT IS STILL DUE!

Respectfully,
Carienomen

Enclosed:
1 brochure, 9978 pages

Untouched by Human Hands

Hellman plucked the last radish out of the can with a pair of dividers. He held it up for Casker to admire, then laid it carefully on the workbench beside the razor.

'Hell of a meal for two grown men,' Casker said, flopping down in one of the ship's padded crash chairs.

'If you'd like to give up your share—' Hellman started to suggest.

Casker shook his head quickly. Hellman smiled, picked up the razor and examined its edge critically.

'Don't make a production out of it,' Casker said, glancing at the ship's instruments. They were approaching a red dwarf, the only planet-bearing sun in the vicinity. 'We want to be through with supper before we get much closer.'

Hellman made a practice incision in the radish, squinting along the top of the razor. Casker bent closer, his mouth open. Hellman poised the razor delicately and cut the radish cleanly in half.

'Will you say grace?' Hellman asked.

Casker growled something and popped a half in his mouth. Hellman chewed more slowly. The sharp taste seemed to explode along his disused tastebuds.

'Not much bulk value,' Hellman said.

Casker didn't answer. He was busily studying the red dwarf.

As he swallowed the last of his radish, Hellman stifled a sigh. Their last meal had been three days ago – if two biscuits and a cup of water could be called a meal. This radish, now resting in the vast emptiness of their stomachs, was the last gram of food on board ship.

'Two planets,' Casker said. 'One's burned to a crisp.'

'Then we'll land on the other.'

Casker nodded and punched a deceleration spiral into the ship's tape.

Hellman found himself wondering for the hundredth time where the fault had been. Could he have made out the food requisitions wrong, when they took on supplies at Calao station? After all, he had been devoting most of his attention to the mining equipment. Or had the ground crew just forgotten to load those last precious cases?

He drew his belt in to the fourth new notch he had punched.

Speculation was useless. Whatever the reason, they were in a jam. Ironically enough, they had more than enough fuel to take them back to Calao. But they would be a pair of singularly emaciated corpses by the time the ship reached there.

'We're coming in now,' Casker said.

And to make matters worse, this unexplored region of space had few suns and fewer planets. Perhaps there was a slight possibility of replenishing their water supply, but the odds were enormous against finding anything they could eat.

'Look at that place!' Casker growled.

Hellman shook himself out of his reverie.

The planet was like a round grey-brown porcupine. The spines of a million needle-sharp mountains glittered in the red dwarf's feeble light. And as they spiralled lower, circling the planet, the pointed mountains seemed to stretch out to meet them.

'It can't be *all* mountains,' Hellman said.

'It's not.'

Sure enough, there were oceans and lakes, out of which thrust jagged island-mountains. But no sign of level land, no hint of civilization, or even animal life.

'At least it's got an oxygen atmosphere,' Casker said.

Their deceleration spiral swept them around the planet, cutting lower into the atmosphere, braking against it. And still there was nothing but mountains and lakes and oceans and more mountains.

On the eighth run, Hellman caught sight of a solitary building on a mountain-top. Casker braked recklessly, and the hull glowed red hot. On the eleventh run, they made a landing approach.

'Stupid place to build,' Casker muttered.

The building was doughnut-shaped, and fitted nicely over the top of the mountain. There was a wide, level lip around it, which Casker scorched as he landed the ship.

From the air, the building had merely seemed big. On the ground, it was enormous. Hellman and Casker walked up to it slowly. Hellman had his burner ready, but there was no sign of life.

'This planet must be abandoned,' Hellman said almost in a whisper.

'Anyone in his right mind would abandon this place,'

89

Casker said. 'There're enough good planets around, without anyone trying to live on a needle point.'

They reached the door. Hellman tried to open it and found it locked. He looked back at the spectacular display of mountains.

'You know,' he said, 'when this planet was still in a molten state, it must have been affected by several gigantic moons that are now broken up. The strains, external and internal, wrenched it into its present spined appearance and—'

'Come off it!' Casker said ungraciously. 'You were a librarian before you decided to get rich on uranium.'

Hellman shrugged his shoulders and burned a hole in the doorlock. They waited.

The only sound on the mountain-top was the growling of their stomachs.

They entered.

The tremendous wedge-shaped room was evidently a warehouse of sorts. Goods were piled to the ceiling, scattered over the floor, stacked haphazardly against the walls. There were boxes and containers of all sizes and shapes, some big enough to hold an elephant, others the size of thimbles.

Near the door was a dusty pile of books. Immediately, Hellman bent down to examine them.

'Must be food somewhere in here,' Casker said, his face lighting up for the first time in a week. He started to open the nearest box.

'This is interesting,' Hellman said, discarding all the books except one.

'Let's eat first!' Casker said, ripping the top off the box.

Inside was a brownish dust. Casker looked at it, sniffed, and made a face.

'Very interesting indeed,' Hellman said, leafing through the book.

Casker opened a small can, which contained a glittering green slime. He closed it and opened another. It contained a dull orange slime.

'Hmm,' Hellman said, still reading.

'Hellman! Will you kindly drop that book and help me find some food?'

'Food?' Hellman repeated, looking up. 'What makes you think there's anything to eat here? For all you know, this could be a paint factory.'

'It's a warehouse,' Casker shouted.

He opened a kidney-shaped can and lifted out a soft purple stick. It hardened quickly and crumpled to dust as he tried to smell it. He scooped up a handful of the dust and brought it to his mouth.

'That might be extract of strychnine,' Hellman said casually.

Casker abruptly dropped the dust and wiped his hands.

'After all,' Hellman pointed out, 'granted that this is a warehouse – a cache, if you wish – we don't know what the late inhabitants considered good fare. Paris Green salad, perhaps, with sulphuric acid as dressing.'

'All right,' Casker said, 'but we gotta eat. What're you going to do about all this?' He gestured at the hundreds of boxes, cans and bottles.

'The thing to do,' Hellman said briskly, 'is to make a qualitative analysis on four or five samples. We could start out with a simple titration, sublimate the chief ingredient, see if it forms a precipitate, work out its molecular make-up from—'

'Hellman, you don't know what you're talking about. You're a librarian, remember? And I'm a correspondence school pilot. We don't know anything about titrations and sublimations.'

'I know,' Hellman said, 'but we should. It's the right way to go about it.'

'Sure. In the meantime, though, just until a chemist drops in, what'll we do?'

'This might help us,' Hellman said, holding up the book. 'Do you know what it is?'

'No,' Casker said, keeping a tight grip on his patience.

'It's a pocket dictionary and guide to the Helg language.'

'Helg?'

'The planet we're on. The symbols match up with those on the boxes.'

Casker raised an eyebrow. 'Never heard of Helg.'

'I don't believe the planet has ever had any contact with Earth,' Hellman said. 'This dictionary isn't Helg–English. It's Helg–Aloombrigian.'

Casker remembered that Aloombrigia was the home planet of a small, adventurous reptilian race, out near the centre of the Galaxy.

'How come you can read Aloombrigian?' Casker asked.

'Oh, being a librarian isn't a completely useless profession,' Hellman said modestly. 'In my spare time—'

'Yeah. Now how about—'

'Do you know,' Hellman said, 'the Aloombrigians

probably helped the Helgans leave their planet and find another. They sell services like that. In which case, this building very likely *is* a food cache!'

'Suppose you start translating,' Casker suggested wearily, 'and maybe find us something to eat.'

They opened boxes until they found a likely-looking substance. Laboriously, Hellman translated the symbols on it.

'Got it,' he said. 'It reads: "USE SNIFFNERS – THE BETTER ABRASIVE."'

'Doesn't sound edible,' Casker said.

'I'm afraid not.'

They found another, which read: VIGROOM! FILL ALL YOUR STOMACHS, AND FILL THEM RIGHT!

'What kind of animals do you suppose these Helgans were?' Casker asked.

Hellman shrugged his shoulders.

The next label took about fifteen minutes to translate. It read: ARGOSEL MAKES YOUR THUDRA ALL TIZZY. CONTAINS THIRTY ARPS OF RAMSTAT PULZ, FOR SHELL LUBRICATION.

'There must be *something* here we can eat,' Casker said with a note of desperation.

'I hope so,' Hellman replied.

At the end of two hours, they were no closer. They had translated dozens of titles and sniffed so many substances that their olfactory senses had given up in disgust.

'Let's talk this over!' Hellman said, sitting on a box marked: VORMITASH – GOOD AS IT SOUNDS!

'Sure,' Casker said, sprawling out on the floor. 'Talk!'

'If we could deduce what kind of creatures inhabited this planet, we'd know what kind of food they ate, and whether it's likely to be edible for us.'

'All we do know is that they wrote a lot of lousy advertising copy.'

Hellman ignored that. 'What kind of intelligent beings would evolve on a planet that is all mountains?'

'Stupid ones,' Casker said.

That was no help. But Hellman found that he couldn't draw any inferences from the mountains. It didn't tell him if the late Helgans ate silicates or proteins or iodine-base foods or anything.

'Now look,' Hellman said, 'we'll have to work this out by pure logic – Are you listening to me?'

'Sure,' Casker said.

'O.K. There's an old proverb that covers our situation perfectly: "One man's meat is another man's poison."'

'Yeah,' Casker said. He was positive his stomach had shrunk to approximately the size of a marble.

'We can assume, first, that their meat is our meat.'

Casker wrenched himself away from a vision of five juicy roast beefs dancing tantalizingly before him. 'What if their meat is our *poison*? What then?'

'Then,' Hellman said, 'we will assume that their poison is our meat.'

'And what happens if their meat *and* their poison are our poison?'

'We starve.'

'All right,' Casker said, standing up. 'Which assumption do we start with?'

'Well, there's no sense in asking for trouble. This *is* an

oxygen planet, if that means anything. Let's assume that we can eat some basic food of theirs. If we can't we'll start on their poisons.'

'If we live that long,' Casker said.

Hellman began to translate labels. They discarded such brands as ANDROGYNITES DELIGHT and VERBELL – FOR LONGER, CURLIER, MORE SENSITIVE ANTENNAE, until they found a small grey box, about six inches by three by three. It was called VALKORIN'S UNIVERSAL TASTE TREAT, FOR ALL DIGESTIVE CAPACITIES.

'This looks as good as any,' Hellman said. He opened the box.

Casker leaned over and sniffed. 'No odour.'

Within the box they found a rectangular, rubbery red block. It quivered slightly, like jelly.

'Bite into it!' Casker said.

'Me?' Hellman asked. 'Why not you?'

'You picked it.'

'I prefer just looking at it,' Hellman said with dignity. 'I'm not hungry.'

'I'm not either,' Casker said.

They sat on the floor and stared at the jelly-like block. After ten minutes, Hellman yawned, leaned back and closed his eyes.

'All right, coward,' Casker said bitterly. 'I'll try it. Just remember, though, if I'm poisoned, you'll never get off this planet! You don't know how to pilot.'

'Just take a little bite, then!' Hellman advised.

Casker leaned over and stared at the block. Then he prodded it with his thumb.

The rubbery red block giggled.

'Did you hear that?' Casker yelped, leaping back.

'I didn't hear anything,' Hellman said, his hands shaking. 'Go ahead!'

Casker prodded the block again. It giggled louder, this time with a disgusting little simper.

'O.K.,' Casker said, 'what do we try next?'

'Next? What's wrong with this?'

'I don't eat anything that giggles,' Casker stated firmly.

'Now listen to me,' Hellman said. 'The creatures who manufactured this might have been trying to create an aesthetic sound as well as a pleasant shape and colour. That giggle is probably only for the amusement of the eater.'

'Then bite into it yourself!' Casker offered.

Hellman glared at him, but made no move towards the rubbery block. Finally he said, 'Let's move it out of the way!'

They pushed the block over to a corner. It lay there giggling softly to itself.

'Now what?' Casker said.

Hellman looked around at the jumbled stacks of incomprehensible alien goods. He noticed a door on either side of the room.

'Let's have a look in the other sections!' he suggested.

Casker shrugged his shoulders apathetically.

Slowly they trudged to the door in the left wall. It was locked and Hellman burned it open with the ship's burner.

It was a wedge-shaped room, piled with incomprehensible alien goods.

The hike back across the room seemed like miles, but they made it only slightly out of wind. Hellman blew out the lock and they looked in.

It was a wedge-shaped room, piled with incomprehensible alien goods.

'All the same,' Casker said sadly, and closed the door.

'Evidently there's a series of these rooms going completely around the building,' Hellman said. 'I wonder if we should explore them?'

Casker calculated the distance around the building, compared it with his remaining strength, and sat down heavily on a long grey object.

'Why bother?' he asked.

Hellman tried to collect his thoughts. Certainly he should be able to find a key of some sort, a clue that would tell him what they could eat. But where was it?

He examined the object Casker was sitting on. It was about the size and shape of a large coffin, with a shallow depression on top. It was made of a hard, corrugated substance.

'What do you suppose this is?' Hellman asked.

'Does it matter?'

Hellman glanced at the symbols painted on the side of the object, then looked them up in his dictionary.

'Fascinating,' he murmured, after a while.

'Is it something to eat?' Casker asked, with a faint glimmering of hope.

'No. You are sitting on something called THE MOROG CUSTOM SUPER TRANSPORT FOR THE DISCRIMINATING HELGAN WHO DESIRES THE BEST IN VERTICAL TRANSPORTATION. It's a vehicle.'

'Oh,' Casker said dully.

'This is important. Look at it! How does it work?'

Casker wearily climbed off the Morog Custom Super

Transport and looked it over carefully. He traced four almost invisible separations on its four corners. 'Retractable wheels, probably, but I don't see—'

Hellman read on. 'It says to give it three amphus of high-gain Integor fuel, then a van of Tonder lubrication, and not to run it over three thousand Ruls for the first fifty mungus.'

'Let's find something to eat!' Casker said.

'Don't you see how important this is?' Hellman asked. 'This could solve our problem. If we could deduce the alien logic inherent in constructing this vehicle, we might know the Helgan thought pattern. This, in turn, would give us an insight into their nervous systems, which would imply their biochemical make-up.'

Casker stood still, trying to decide whether he had enough strength left to strangle Hellman.

'For example,' Hellman said, 'what kind of vehicle would be used in a place like this? Not one with wheels, since everything is up and down. Anti-gravity? Perhaps, but what *kind* of anti-gravity? And why did the inhabitants devise a box-like form instead—'

Casker decided sadly that he didn't have enough strength to strangle Hellman, no matter how pleasant it might be. Very quietly, he said, 'Kindly stop making like a scientist! Let's see if there isn't *something* we can gulp down!'

'All right,' Hellman said sulkily.

Casker watched his partner wander off among the cans, bottles and cases. He wondered vaguely where Hellman got the energy, and decided that he was just too cerebral to know when he was starving.

'Here's something,' Hellman called out, standing in front of a large yellow vat.

'What does it say?' Casker asked.

'Little bit hard to translate. But rendered freely, it reads: MORISHILLE'S VOOZY, WITH LACTO-ECTO ADDED FOR A NEW TASTE SENSATION. EVERYONE DRINKS VOOZY. GOOD BEFORE AND AFTER MEALS, NO UNPLEASANT AFTER-EFFECTS. GOOD FOR CHILDREN. THE DRINK OF THE UNIVERSE.'

'That sounds good,' Casker admitted, thinking that Hellman might not be so stupid after all.

'This should tell us once and for all if their meat *is* our meat,' Hellman said. 'This Voozy seems to be the closest thing to a universal drink I've found yet.'

'Maybe,' Casker said hopefully, 'maybe it's just plain water?'

'We'll see.' Hellman pried open the lid with the edge of the burner.

Within the vat was a crystal-clear liquid.

'No odour,' Casker said, bending over the vat.

The crystal liquid lifted to meet him.

Casker retreated so rapidly that he fell over a box. Hellman helped him to his feet, and they approached the vat again. As they came near, the liquid lifted itself three feet into the air and moved towards them.

'What've you done now?' Casker asked, moving back carefully. The liquid flowed slowly over the side of the vat. It began to flow towards him.

'Hellman!' Casker shrieked.

Hellman was standing to one side perspiration pouring down his face, reading his dictionary with a preoccupied frown.

'Guess I bumbled the translation,' he said.

'Do something!' Casker shouted. The liquid was trying to back him into a corner.

'Nothing I can do,' Hellman said, reading on. 'Ah, here's the error. It doesn't say "Everyone drinks Voozy." Wrong subject. "Voozy drinks *everyone*." That tells us something! The Helgans must have soaked liquid in through their pores. Naturally, they would prefer to be drunk, instead of to drink.'

Casker tried to dodge around the liquid, but it cut him off with a merry gurgle. Desperately he picked up a small bale and threw it at the Voozy. The Voozy caught the bale and drank it. Then it discarded that and turned back to Casker.

Hellman tossed another box. The Voozy drank this one and a third and fourth that Casker threw in. Then, apparently exhausted, it flowed back into its vat.

Casker clapped down the lid and sat on it, trembling violently.

'Not so good,' Hellman said. 'We've been taking it for granted that the Helgans had eating habits like us. But, of course, it doesn't necessarily—'

'No, it doesn't. No, sir, it certainly doesn't. I guess we can see that it doesn't. Anyone can see that it doesn't—'

'Stop that!' Hellman ordered sternly. 'We've no time for hysteria.'

'Sorry.' Casker slowly moved away from the Voozy vat.

'I guess we'll have to assume that their meat is our poison,' Hellman said thoughtfully. 'So now we'll see if their poison is our meat.'

Casker didn't say anything. He was wondering what would have happened if the Voozy had drunk him.

In the corner, the rubbery block was still giggling to itself.

'Now here's a likely-looking poison,' Hellman said, half an hour later.

Casker had recovered completely, except for an occasional twitch of the lips.

'What does it say?' he asked.

Hellman rolled a tiny tube in the palm of his hand. 'It's called Pvastkin's Plugger. The label reads: WARNING! HIGHLY DANGEROUS! PVASTKIN'S PLUGGER IS DESIGNED TO FILL HOLES OR CRACKS OF NOT MORE THAN TWO CUBIC VIMS. HOWEVER — THE PLUGGER IS NOT TO BE EATEN UNDER ANY CIRCUMSTANCES. THE ACTIVE INGREDIENT, RAMOTOL, WHICH MAKES PVASTKIN'S SO EXCELLENT A PLUGGER, RENDERS IT HIGHLY DANGEROUS WHEN TAKEN INTERNALLY.'

'Sounds great,' Casker said. 'It'll probably blow us sky-high.'

'Do you have any other suggestions?' Hellman asked.

Casker thought for a moment. The food of Helg was obviously unpalatable for humans. So perhaps was their poison . . . but wasn't starvation better than this sort of thing?

After a moment's communion with his stomach, he decided that starvation was *not* better.

'Go ahead,' he said.

Hellman slipped the burner under his arm and unscrewed the top of the little bottle. He shook it.

Nothing happened.

'It's got a seal,' Casker pointed out.

Hellman punctured the seal with his fingernail and set the bottle on the floor. An evil-smelling green froth began to bubble out.

Hellman looked dubiously at the froth. It was congealing into a glob and spreading over the floor.

'Yeast, perhaps,' he said, gripping the burner tightly.

'Come, come. Faint heart never filled empty stomach.'

'I'm not holding *you* back,' Hellman said.

The glob swelled to the size of a man's head.

'How long is that supposed to go on?' Casker asked.

'Well,' Hellman said, 'it's advertised as a Plugger. I suppose that's what it does – expands to plug up holes.'

'Sure. But how *much*?'

'Unfortunately, I don't know how much two cubic vims are. But it can't go on much—'

Belatedly, they noticed that the Plugger had filled almost a quarter of the room and was showing no signs of stopping.

'We should have believed the label!' Casker yelled to him, across the spreading glob. 'It *is* dangerous!'

As the Plugger produced more surface, it began to accelerate in its growth. A sticky edge touched Hellman and he jumped back.

'Watch out!'

He couldn't reach Casker, on the other side of the gigantic sphere of blob. Hellman tried to run around, but the Plugger had spread, cutting the room in half. It began to swell towards the walls.

'Run for it!' Hellman yelled, and rushed to the door behind him.

He flung it open just as the expanding glob reached him. On the other side of the room he heard a door slam shut. Hellman didn't wait any longer. He sprinted through and slammed the door behind him.

He stood for a moment, panting, the burner in his hand. He hadn't realized how weak he was. That sprint had cut his reserves of energy dangerously close to the collapsing point. At least Casker had made it, too, though.

But he was still in trouble.

The Plugger poured merrily through the blasted lock, into the room. Hellman tried a practice shot on it, but the Plugger was evidently impervious . . . as, he realized, a good plugger should be.

It was showing no signs of fatigue.

Hellman hurried to the far wall. The door was locked, as the others had been, so he burned out the lock and went through.

How far could the glob expand? How much was two cubic vims? Two cubic miles, perhaps? For all he knew, the Plugger was used to repair faults in the crusts of planets.

In the next room, Hellman stopped to catch his breath. He remembered that the building was circular. He would burn his way through the remaining doors and join Casker. They would burn their way outside and—

Casker didn't have a burner.

Hellman turned white with shock. Casker had made it into the room on the right, because they had burned it open earlier. The Plugger was undoubtedly oozing into that room, through the shattered lock – and Casker couldn't get out. The Plugger was on his left, a locked door on his right.

Rallying his remaining strength, Hellman began to run. Boxes seemed to get in his way purposefully, tripping him, slowing him down. He blasted the next door and hurried on to the next. And the next. And the next.

The Plugger couldn't expand *completely* into Casker's room.

Or could it?

The wedge-shaped rooms, each a segment of a circle, seemed to stretch before him for ever, a jumbled montage of locked doors, alien goods, more doors, more goods. Hellman fell over a crate, got to his feet and fell again. He had reached the limit of his strength, and passed it. But Casker was his friend.

Besides, without a pilot, he'd never get off the place.

Hellman struggled through two more rooms on trembling legs and then collapsed in front of a third.

'Is that you, Hellman?' he heard Casker ask, from the other side of the door.

'You all right?' Hellman managed to gasp.

'Haven't much room in here,' Casker said, 'but the Plugger's stopped growing. Hellman, get me out of here!'

Hellman lay on the floor panting. 'Moment,' he said.

'Moment, hell!' Casker shouted. 'Get me out! I've found water.'

'What? How?'

'Get me out of here!'

Hellman tried to stand up, but his legs weren't co-operating. 'What happened?' he asked.

'When I saw that glob filling the room, I figured I'd try to start up the Super Custom Transport. Thought maybe it could knock down the door and get me out. So I pumped it full of high-gain Integor fuel.'

'Yes?' Hellman said, still trying to get his legs under control.

'That Super Custom Transport is an animal, Hellman! And the Integor fuel is water. Now get me out!'

Hellman lay back with a contented sigh. If he had had a little more time, he would have worked out the whole thing himself, by pure logic. But it was all very apparent now. The most efficient machine to go over those vertical, razor-sharp mountains would be an animal, probably with retractable suckers. It was kept in hibernation between trips; and if it drank water, the other products designed for it would be palatable, too. Of course they still didn't know much about the late inhabitants, but undoubtedly—

'Burn down that door!' Casker shrieked, his voice breaking.

Hellman was pondering the irony of it all. If one man's meat – *and* his poison – are your poison, then try eating something else. So simple, really.

But there was one thing that still bothered him.

'How did you know it was an Earth-type animal?' he asked.

'Its breath, stupid! It inhales and exhales and smells as if it's eaten onions.' There was a sound of cans falling and bottles shattering. 'Now hurry!'

'What's wrong?' Hellman asked, finally getting to his feet and poising the burner.

'The Custom Super Transport. It's got me cornered behind a pile of cases. Hellman, it seems to think that I'm *its* meat!'

Watchbird

When Gelsen entered, he saw that the rest of the watchbird manufacturers were already present. There were six of them, not counting himself, and the room was blue with expensive cigar smoke.

'Hi, Charlie!' one of them called as he came in.

The rest broke off conversation long enough to wave a casual greeting at him. As a watchbird manufacturer, he was a member manufacturer of salvation, he reminded himself wryly. Very exclusive. You must have a certified government contract if you want to save the human race.

'The government representative isn't here yet,' one of the men told him. 'He's due any minute.'

'We're getting the green light,' another said.

'Fine.' Gelsen found a chair near the door and looked around the room. It was like a convention, or a Boy Scout rally. The six men made up for their lack of numbers by sheer volume. The president of Southern Consolidated was talking at the top of his lungs about watchbird's enormous durability. The two presidents he was talking at were grinning, nodding, one trying to interrupt with the results of a test he had run on watchbird's resourcefulness, the other talking about the new recharging apparatus.

The other three men were in their own little group, delivering what sounded like a panegyric to watchbird.

Gelsen noticed that all of them stood straight and tall,

like the saviours they felt they were. He didn't find it funny. Up to a few days ago he had felt that way himself. He had considered himself a pot-bellied, slightly balding saint.

He sighed and lighted a cigarette. At the beginning of the project, he had been as enthusiastic as the others. He remembered saying to Macintyre, his chief engineer, 'Mac, a new day is coming. Watchbird is the Answer.' And Macintyre had nodded very profoundly – another watchbird convert.

How wonderful it had seemed then! A simple, reliable answer to one of mankind's greatest problems, all wrapped and packaged in a pound of incorruptible metal, crystal and plastics.

Perhaps that was the very reason he was doubting it now. Gelsen suspected that you don't solve human problems so easily. There had to be a catch somewhere.

After all, murder was an old problem, and watchbird too new a solution.

'Gentlemen—' They had been talking so heatedly that they hadn't noticed the government representative entering. Now the room became quiet at once.

'Gentlemen,' the plump government man said, 'the President, with the consent of Congress, has acted to form a watchbird division for every city and town in the country.'

The men burst into a spontaneous shout of triumph. They were going to have their chance to save the world after all, Gelsen thought, and worriedly asked himself what was wrong with that.

He listened carefully as the government man outlined

the distribution scheme. The country was to be divided into seven areas, each to be supplied and serviced by one manufacturer. This meant monopoly, of course, but a necessary one. Like the telephone service, it was in the public's best interests. You couldn't have competition in watchbird service. Watchbird was for everyone.

'The President hopes,' the representative continued, 'that full watchbird service will be installed in the shortest possible time. You will have top priorities on strategic metals, manpower, and so forth.'

'Speaking for myself,' the president of Southern Consolidated said, 'I expect to have the first batch: of watchbirds distributed within the week. Production is all set up.'

The rest of the men were equally ready. The factories had been prepared to roll out the watchbirds for months now. The final standardized equipment had been agreed upon, and only the Presidential go-ahead had been lacking.

'Fine,' the representative said. 'If that is all, I think we can – is there a question?'

'Yes, sir,' Gelsen said. 'I want to know if the present model is the one we are going to manufacture.'

'Of course,' the representative said. 'It's the most advanced.'

'I have an objection.' Gelsen stood up. His colleagues were glaring coldly at him. Obviously he was delaying the advent of the golden age.

'What is your objection?' the representative asked.

'First, let me say that I am one hundred per cent in favour of a machine to stop murder. It's been needed for a long time. I object only to the watchbird's learning circuits. They serve, in effect, to animate the machine and give it a pseudo-consciousness. I can't approve of that.'

'But, Mr Gelsen, you yourself testified that the watchbird would not be completely efficient unless such circuits were introduced. Without them, the watchbirds could stop only an estimated seventy per cent of murders.'

'I know that,' Gelsen said, feeling extremely uncomfortable. 'I believe there might be a moral danger in allowing a machine to make decisions that are rightfully Man's,' he declared doggedly.

'Oh, come now, Gelsen!' one of the corporation presidents said. 'It's nothing of the sort. The watchbird will only reinforce the decisions made by honest men from the beginning of time.'

'I think that is true,' the representative agreed. 'But I can understand how Mr. Gelsen feels. It is sad that we must put a human problem into the hands of a machine, sadder still that we must have a machine enforce our laws. But I ask you to remember, Mr. Gelsen, that there is no other possible way of stopping a murderer *before he strikes*. It would be unfair to the many innocent people killed every year if we were to restrict watchbird on philosophical grounds. Don't you agree that I'm right?'

'Yes, I suppose I do,' Gelsen said unhappily. He had told himself all that a thousand times, but something still bothered him. Perhaps he would talk it over with Macintyre.

As the conference broke up, a thought struck him. He grinned.

A lot of policemen were going to be out of work.

*

'Now what do you think of that?' Officer Celtrics demanded. 'Fifteen years in Homicide and a machine is replacing me.' He wiped a large red hand across his forehead and leaned against the captain's desk. 'Ain't science marvellous?'

Two other policemen, late of Homicide, nodded glumly.

'Don't worry about it!' the captain said. 'We'll find a home for you in Larceny, Celtrics. You'll like it here.'

'I just can't get over it,' Celtrics complained. 'A lousy little piece of tin and glass is going to solve all the crimes.'

'Not quite,' the captain said. 'The watchbirds are supposed to prevent the crimes before they happen.'

'Then how'll they be crimes?' one of the policemen asked. 'I mean they can't hang you for murder until you commit one, can they?'

'That's not the idea,' the captain said. 'The watchbirds are supposed to stop a man before he commits a murder.'

'Then no one arrests him?' Celtrics asked.

'I don't know how they're going to work that out,' the captain admitted.

The men were silent for a while. The captain yawned and examined his watch.

'The thing I don't understand,' Celtrics said, still leaning on the captain's desk, 'is just how do they do it? How did it start, Captain?'

The captain studied Celtrics' face for possible irony; after all, watchbird had been in the papers for months. But then he remembered that Celtrics, like his sidekicks, rarely bothered to turn past the sports pages.

'Well,' the captain said, trying to remember what he had read in the Sunday supplements, 'these scientists were working on criminology. They were studying murderers, to find out what made them tick. So they found that murderers throw out a different sort of brain wave from ordinary people. And their glands act funny, too. All this happens when they're about to commit a murder. So these scientists worked out a special machine to flash red or something when these brain waves turned on.'

'Scientists,' Celtrics said bitterly.

'Well, after the scientists had this machine, they didn't know what to do with it. It was too big to move around, and murderers didn't drop in often enough to make it flash. So they built it into a smaller unit and tried it out in a few police stations. I think they tried one upstate. But it didn't work so good. You couldn't get to the crime in time. That's why they built the watchbirds.'

'I don't think they'll stop no criminals,' one of the policemen insisted.

'They sure will. I read the test results. They can smell him out before he commits a crime. And when they reach him, they give him a powerful shock or something. It'll stop him.'

'You closing up Homicide, Captain?' Celtrics asked.

'Nope,' the captain said. 'I'm leaving a skeleton crew in until we see how these birds do.'

'Hah!' Celtrics said. 'Skeleton crew! That's funny.'

'Sure,' the captain said. 'Anyhow, I'm going to leave some men on. It seems the birds don't stop all murders.'

'Why not?'

'Some murderers don't have these brain waves,' the captain answered, trying to remember what the newspaper article had said. 'Or their glands don't work or something.'

'Which ones don't they stop?' Celtrics asked, with professional curiosity.

'I don't know. But I hear they got the damned things fixed so they're going to stop all of them soon.'

'How they working that?'

'They learn. The watchbirds, I mean. Just like people.'

'You kidding me?'

'Nope.'

'Well,' Celtrics said, 'I think I'll just keep old Betsy oiled, just in case. You can't trust these scientists.'

'Right.'

'Birds!' Celtrics scoffed.

Over the town, the watchbird soared in a long, lazy curve. Its aluminium hide glistened in the morning sun, and dots of light danced on its stiff wings. Silently it flew.

Silently, but with all senses functioning. Built-in kinaesthetics told the watchbird where it was, and held it in a long search curve. Its eyes and ears operated as one unit, searching, seeking.

And then something happened. The watchbird's electronically fast reflexes picked up the edge of a sensation. A correlation centre tested it, matching it with electrical and chemical data in its memory files. A relay tripped.

Down the watchbird spiralled, coming in on the

increasingly strong sensation. It *smelled* the outpouring of certain glands, *tasted* a deviant brain wave.

Fully alerted and armed, it spun and banked in the bright morning sunlight.

Dinelli was so intent he didn't see the watchbird coming. He had his gun poised, and his eyes pleaded with the big grocer.

'Don't come no closer!'

'You lousy little punk,' the grocer said, and took another step forward. 'Rob me? I'll break every bone in your puny body.'

The grocer, too stupid or too courageous to understand the threat of the gun, advanced on the little thief.

'All right,' Dinelli said, in a thorough state of panic. 'All right, sucker, take—'

A bolt of electricity knocked him on his back. The gun went off, smashing a breakfast food display.

'What in hell?' the grocer asked, staring at the stunned thief. And then he saw a flash of silver wings. 'Well, I'm really damned. Those watchbirds work.'

He stared until the wings disappeared in the sky. Then he telephoned the police.

The watchbird returned to his search curve. His thinking centre correlated the new facts he had learned about murder. Several of these he hadn't known before.

This new information was simultaneously flashed to all the other watchbirds and their information was flashed back to him.

New information, methods, definitions were constantly passing between them.

*

Now that the watchbirds were rolling off the assembly line in a steady stream, Gelsen allowed himself to relax. A loud contented hum filled his plant. Orders were being filled on time, with top priorities given to the biggest cities in his area, and working down to the smallest towns.

'All smooth, Chief,' Macintyre said, coming in the door. He had just completed a routine inspection.

'Fine. Have a seat!'

The big engineer sat down and lighted a cigarette.

'We've been working on this for some time,' Gelsen said, when he couldn't think of anything else.

'We sure have,' Macintyre agreed. He leaned back and inhaled deeply. He had been one of the consulting engineers on the original watchbird. That was six years back. He had been working for Gelsen ever since, and the men had become good friends.

'The thing I wanted to ask you was this—' Gelsen paused. He couldn't think how to phrase what he wanted. Instead he asked, 'What do you think of the watchbirds, Mac?'

'Who, me?' The engineer grinned nervously. He had been eating, drinking and sleeping watchbird ever since its inception. He had never found it necessary to have an attitude. 'Why, I think it's great.'

'I don't mean that,' Gelsen said. He realised that what he wanted was to have someone understand his point of view. 'I mean do you figure there might be some danger in machine thinking?'

'I don't think so, Chief. Why do you ask?'

'Look, I'm no scientist or engineer. I've just handled

cost and production and let you boys worry about how. But as a layman, watchbird is starting to frighten me.'

'No reason for that.'

'I don't like the idea of the learning circuits.'

'But why not?' Then Macintyre grinned again. 'I know. You're like a lot of people, Chief – afraid your machines are going to wake up and say, "What are we doing here? Let's go out and rule the world." Is that it?'

'Maybe something like that,' Gelsen admitted.

'No chance of it,' Macintyre said. 'The watchbirds are complex, I'll admit, but an M. I. T. calculator is a whole lot more complex. And it hasn't got consciousness.'

'No. But the watchbirds can *learn*.'

'Sure. So can all the new calculators. Do you think they'll team up with the watchbirds?'

Gelsen felt annoyed at Macintyre, and even more annoyed at himself for being ridiculous. 'It's a fact that the watch-birds can put their learning into action. No one is monitoring them.'

'So that's the trouble,' Macintyre said.

'I've been thinking of getting out of watchbird.' Gelsen hadn't realized it until that moment.

'Look, Chief,' Macintyre said. 'Will you take an engineer's word on this?'

'Let's hear it.'

'The watchbirds are no more dangerous than an auto-mobile, an IBM calculator or a thermometer. They have no more consciousness or volition than those things. The watchbirds are built to respond to certain stimuli, and to carry out certain operations when they receive that stimuli.'

'And the learning circuits?'

'You have to have those,' Macintyre said patiently, as though explaining the whole thing to a ten-year-old. 'The purpose of the watchbird is to frustrate all murder-attempts, right? Well, only certain murderers give out these stimuli. In order to stop all of them, the watchbird has to search out new definitions of murder and correlate them with what it already knows.'

'I think it's inhuman,' Gelsen said.

'That's the best thing about it. The watchbirds are unemotional. Their reasoning is non-anthropomorphic. You can't bribe them or drug them. You shouldn't fear them, either.'

The intercom on Gelsen's desk buzzed. He ignored it.

'I know all this,' Gelsen said. 'But, still, sometimes I feel like the man who invented dynamite. He thought it would only be used for blowing up tree stumps.'

'*You* didn't invent watchbird.'

'I still feel morally responsible because I manufacture them.'

The intercom buzzed again, and Gelsen irritably punched a button.

'The reports are in on the first week of watchbird operation,' his secretary told him.

'How do they look?'

'Wonderful, sir.'

'Send them in in fifteen minutes.' Gelsen switched the intercom off and turned back to Macintyre, who was

117

cleaning his fingernails with a wooden match. 'Don't you think that this represents a trend in human thinking? The mechanical god? The electronic father?'

'Chief,' Macintyre said, 'I think you should study watchbird more closely. Do you know what's built into the circuits?'

'Only generally.'

'First, there is a purpose. Which is to stop living organisms from committing murder. Two, murder may be defined as an act of violence, consisting of breaking, mangling, maltreating or otherwise stopping the functions of a living organism by a living organism. Three, most murderers are detectable by certain chemical and electrical changes.'

Macintyre paused to light another cigarette. 'Those conditions take care of the routine functions. Then, for the learning circuits, there are two more conditions. Four, there are some living organisms who commit murder without the signs mentioned in three. Five, these can be detected by data applicable to condition two.'

'I see,' Gelsen said.

'You realise how foolproof it is?'

'I suppose so.' Gelsen hesitated a moment. 'I guess that's all.'

'Right,' the engineer said, and left.

Gelsen thought for a few moments. There *couldn't* be anything wrong with the watchbirds.

'Send in the reports!' he said into the intercom.

High above the lighted buildings of the city, the watchbird soared. It was dark, but in the distance the watchbird could see another, and another beyond that. For this was a large city.

To prevent murder . . .

There was more to watch for now. New information had crossed the invisible network that connected all watchbirds. New data, new ways of detecting the violence of murder.

There! The edge of a sensation! Two watchbirds dipped simultaneously. One had received the scent a fraction of a second before the other. He continued down while the other resumed monitoring.

Condition four, there are some living organisms who commit murder without the signs mentioned in condition three.

Through his new information, the watchbird knew by extrapolation that this organism was bent on murder, even though the characteristic chemical and electrical smells were absent.

The watchbird, all senses acute, closed in on the organism. He found what he wanted, and dived.

Roger Greco leaned against a building, his hands in his pockets. In his left hand was the cool butt of a .45. Greco waited patiently.

He wasn't thinking of anything in particular, just relaxing against a building, waiting for a man. Greco didn't know why the man was to be killed. He didn't care. Greco's lack of curiosity was part of his value. The other part was his skill.

One bullet, neatly placed in the head of a man he didn't know. It didn't excite him or sicken him. It was a job, just like anything else. You killed a man. So?

As Greco's victim stepped out of a building, Greco

lifted the .45 out of his pocket. He released the safety and braced the gun with his right hand. He still wasn't thinking of anything as he took aim . . .

And was knocked off his feet.

Greco thought he had been shot. He struggled up again, looked around, and sighted foggily on his victim.

Again he was knocked down.

This time he lay on the ground, trying to draw a bead. He never thought of stopping, for Greco was a craftsman.

With the next blow, everything went black. Permanently, because the watchbird's duty was to protect the object of violence – *at whatever cost to the murderer.*

The victim walked to his car. He hadn't noticed anything unusual. Everything had happened in silence.

Gelsen was feeling pretty good. The watchbirds had been operating perfectly. Crimes of violence had been cut in half, and cut again. Dark alleys were no longer mouths of horror. Parks and playgrounds were not places to shun after dusk.

Of course, there were still robberies. Petty thievery flourished, and embezzlement, larceny, forgery and a hundred other crimes.

But that wasn't so important. You could regain lost money – never a lost life.

Gelsen was ready to admit that he had been wrong about the watchbirds. They *were* doing a job that humans had been unable to accomplish.

The first hint of something wrong came that morning. Macintyre came into his office. He stood silently in front of Gelsen's desk, looking annoyed and a little embarrassed.

'What's the matter, Mac?' Gelsen asked.

'One of the watchbirds went to work on a slaughter-house man. Knocked him out.'

Gelsen thought about it for a moment. Yes, the watchbirds would do that. With their new learning circuits, they had probably defined the killing of animals as murder.

'Tell the packers to mechanize their slaughtering,' Gelsen said. 'I never liked that business myself.'

'All right,' Macintyre said. He pursed his lips, then shrugged his shoulders and left.

Gelsen stood beside his desk, thinking. Couldn't the watchbirds differentiate between a murderer and a man engaged in a legitimate profession? No, evidently not. To them, murder was murder. No exceptions. He frowned. That might take a little ironing out in the circuits.

But not too much, he decided hastily. Just make them a little more discriminating.

He sat down again and buried himself in paperwork, trying to avoid the edge of an old fear.

They strapped the prisoner into the chair and fitted the electrode to his leg.

'Oh, oh,' he moaned, only half-conscious now of what they were doing.

They fitted the helmet over his shaved head and tightened the last straps. He continued to moan softly.

And then the watchbird swept in. How he had come, no one knew. Prisons are large and strong, with many locked doors, but the watchbird was there—

To stop a murder.

'Get that thing out of here!' the warden shouted, and reached for the switch. The watchbird knocked him down.

'Stop that!' a guard screamed, and grabbed for the switch himself. He was knocked to the floor beside the warden.

'This isn't murder, you idiot!' another guard said. He drew his gun to shoot down the glittering, wheeling metal bird.

Anticipating, the watchbird smashed him back against the wall.

There was silence in the room. After a while, the man in the helmet started to giggle. Then he stopped.

The watchbird stood on guard, fluttering in mid-air—
Making sure no murder was done.

New data flashed along the watchbird network.

Unmonitored, independent, the thousands of watchbirds received and acted upon it.

The breaking, mangling or otherwise stopping the functions of a living organism by a living organism. New acts to stop.

'Damn you, git going!' Farmer Ollister shouted, and raised his whip again. The horse balked, and the wagon rattled and shook as he edged sideways.

'You lousy hunk of pigmeal, git going!' the farmer yelled and he raised the whip again.

It never fell. An alert watchbird, sensing violence, had knocked him out of his seat.

A living organism? What is a living organism? The watchbirds extended their definitions as they became aware of more facts. And, of course, this gave them more work.

The deer was just visible at the edge of the woods. The hunter raised his rifle, and took careful aim.

He didn't have time to shoot.

With his free hand, Gelsen mopped perspiration from his face. 'All right,' he said into the telephone. He listened to the stream of vituperation from the other end, then placed the receiver gently in its cradle.

'What was that one?' Macintyre asked. He was unshaven, tie loose, shirt unbuttoned.

'Another fisherman,' Gelsen said. 'It seems the watchbirds won't let him fish even though his family is starving. What are we going to do about it, he wants to know.'

'How many hundred is that?'

'I don't know. I haven't opened the mail.'

'Well, I figured out where the trouble is,' Macintyre said gloomily, with the air of a man who knows just how he blew up the Earth – after it was too late.

'Let's hear it.'

'Everybody took it for granted that we wanted all murder stopped. We figured the watchbirds would think as we do. We ought to have qualified the conditions.'

'I've got an idea,' Gelsen said, 'that we'd have to know just why and what murder is, before we could qualify the conditions properly. And if we knew that, we wouldn't need the watchbirds.'

'Oh, I don't know about that. They just have to be told that some things which look like murder are not murder.'

'But why should they stop fishermen?' Gelsen asked.

'Why shouldn't they? Fish and animals are living organisms. We just don't think that killing them is murder.'

The telephone rang. Gelsen glared at it and punched the intercom. 'I told you no more calls, no matter what.'

'This is from Washington,' his secretary said. 'I thought you'd—'

'Sorry.' Gelsen picked up the telephone. 'Yes. Certainly is a mess. . . . Have they? All right, I certainly will.' He put down the telephone.

'Short and sweet,' he told Macintyre. 'We're to shut down temporarily.'

'That won't be so easy,' Macintyre said. 'The watchbirds operate independent of any central control, you know. They come back once a week for a repair checkup. We'll have to turn them off then, one by one.'

'Well, let's get to it. Monroe over on the Coast has shut down about a quarter of his birds.'

'I think I can dope out a restricting circuit,' Macintyre said.

'Fine,' Gelsen replied bitterly. 'You make me very happy.'

The watchbirds were learning rapidly, expanding and adding to their knowledge. Loosely defined abstractions were extended, acted upon and re-extended.

To stop murder . . .

Metal and electrons reason well, but not in a human fashion.

A living organism? Any living organism.

The watchbirds set themselves the task of protecting all living things.

The fly buzzed around the room, lighting on a table top, pausing a moment, then darting to a window-sill.

The old man stalked it, a rolled newspaper in his hand.

Murderer!

The watchbirds swept down and saved the fly in the nick of time.

The old man writhed on the floor a minute and then was silent. He had been given only a mild shock, but it had been enough for his fluttery, cranky heart.

His victim had been saved, though, and this was the important thing. Save the victim and give the aggressor his just deserts.

Gelsen demanded angrily, 'Why aren't they being turned off?'

The assistant control engineer gestured. In a corner of the repair room lay the senior control engineer. He was just regaining consciousness.

'He tried to turn one of them off,' the assistant engineer said. Both his hands were knotted together. He was making a visible effort not to shake.

'That's ridiculous. They haven't got any sense of self-preservation.'

'Then turn them off yourself! Besides, I don't think any more are going to come.'

What could have happened? Gelsen began to piece it together. The watchbirds still hadn't decided on the limits of a living organism. When some of them were turned off in the Monroe plant, the rest must have correlated the data.

So they had been forced to assume that they were living organisms, as well.

No one had ever told them otherwise. Certainly they carried on most of the functions of living organisms.

Then the old fears hit him. Gelsen trembled and hurried out of the repair room. He wanted to find Macintyre in a hurry.

The nurse handed the surgeon the sponge.

'Scalpel.'

She placed it in his hand. He started to make the first incision. And then he was aware of a disturbance.

'Who let that thing in?'

'I don't know,' the nurse said, her voice muffled by the mask.

'Get it out of here!'

The nurse waved her arms at the bright winged thing, but it fluttered over her head.

The surgeon proceeded with the incision – as long as he was able.

The watchbird drove him away and stood guard.

'Telephone the watchbird company!' the surgeon ordered. 'Get them to turn the thing off!'

The watchbird was preventing violence to a living organism.

The surgeon stood by helplessly while his patient died.

Fluttering high above the network of highways, the watchbird watched and waited. It had been constantly working for weeks now, without rest or repair. Rest and repair were impossible, because the watchbird couldn't allow itself – a living organism – to be murdered. And that was what happened when watchbirds returned to the factory.

There was a built-in order to return, after the lapse of a certain time period. But the watchbird had a stronger order to obey – preservation of life, including its own.

The definitions of murder were almost infinitely extended now, impossible to cope with. But the watchbird didn't consider that. It responded to its stimuli, whenever they came and whatever their source.

There was a new definition of living organism in its memory files. It had come as a result of the watchbird discovery that watchbirds were living organisms. And it had enormous ramifications.

The stimuli came. For the hundredth time that day, the bird wheeled and banked, dropping swiftly down to stop murder.

Jackson yawned and pulled his car to a shoulder of the road. He didn't notice the glittering dot in the sky. There was no reason for him to. Jackson wasn't contemplating murder, by any human definition.

This was a good spot for a nap, he decided. He had been driving for seven straight hours and his eyes were starting to fog. He reached out to turn off the ignition key—

And was knocked back against the side of the car.

'What in hell's wrong with you?' he asked indignantly. 'All I want to do is—' He reached for the key again, and again he was smacked back.

Jackson knew better than to try a third time. He had been listening to the radio and he knew what the watchbirds did to stubborn violators.

'You mechanical jerk,' he said to the waiting metal bird. 'A car's not alive. I'm not trying to kill it.'

But the watchbird only knew that a certain operation resulted in stopping an organism. The car was certainly a functioning organism. Wasn't it of metal, as were the watchbirds? Didn't it run?

Macintyre said, 'Without repairs they'll run down.' He shoved a pile of specification sheets out of his way.

'How soon?' Gelsen asked.

'Six months to a year. Say a year, barring accidents.'

'A year,' Gelsen said. 'In the meantime, everything is stopping dead. Do you know the latest?'

'What?'

'The watchbirds have decided that the Earth is a living organism. They won't allow farmers to break ground for ploughing. And, of course, everything else is a living organism – rabbits, beetles, flies, wolves, mosquitoes, lions, crocodiles, crows, and smaller forms of life such as bacteria.'

'I know,' Macintyre said.

'And you tell me they'll wear out in six months or a year. What happens *now*? What are we going to eat in six months?'

The engineer rubbed his chin. 'We'll have to do something quick and fast. Ecological balance is gone to hell.'

'Fast isn't the word. Instantaneously would be better.' Gelsen lighted his thirty-fifth cigarette for the day. 'At least I have the bitter satisfaction of saying, "I told you so." Although I'm just as responsible as the rest of the machine-worshipping fools.'

Macintyre wasn't listening. He was thinking about watchbirds. 'Like the rabbit plague in Australia.'

'The death rate is mounting,' Gelsen said. 'Famine. Floods. Can't cut down trees. Doctors can't – what was that you said about Australia?'

'The rabbits,' Macintyre repeated. 'Hardly any left in Australia now.'

'Why? How was it done?'

'Oh, found some kind of germ that attacked only rabbits. I think it was propagated by mosquitoes—'

'Work on that,' Gelsen said. 'You might have something. I want you to get on the telephone, ask for an emergency hook-up with the engineers of the other companies. Hurry it up. Together you may be able to dope out something.'

'Right,' Macintyre said. He grabbed a handful of blank paper and hurried to the telephone.

'What did I tell you?' Officer Celtrics said. He grinned at the captain. 'Didn't I tell you scientists were nuts?'

'I didn't say you were wrong, did I?' the captain asked.

'No, but you weren't *sure*.'

'Well, I'm sure now. You'd better get going. There's plenty of work for you.'

'I know.' Celtrics drew his revolver from its holster, checked it and put it back. 'Are all the boys back, Captain?'

'All?' the captain laughed humourlessly. 'Homicide has increased by fifty per cent. There's more murder now than there's ever been.'

'Sure,' Celtrics said. 'The watchbirds are too busy guarding cars and slugging spiders.' He started towards the door, then turned for a parting shot.

'Take my word, Captain. Machines are *stupid*.'

The captain nodded.

Thousands of watchbirds, trying to stop countless millions of murders – a hopeless task. But the watchbirds didn't hope. Without consciousness, they experienced no sense of accomplishment, no fear of failure. Patiently they went about their jobs, obeying each stimulus as it came.

They couldn't be everywhere at the same time, but it wasn't necessary to be. People learned quickly what the watchbirds didn't like and refrained from doing it.

It just wasn't safe. With their high speed and superfast senses, the watchbirds got around quickly.

And now they meant business. In their original directives there had been a provision made for killing a murderer, if all other means failed.

Why spare a murderer?

It backfired. The watchbirds extracted the fact that murder and crimes of violence had increased geometrically since they had begun operation. This was true, because their new definitions increased the possibilities of murder. But to the watchbirds, the rise showed that the first methods had failed.

Simple logic. If A doesn't work, try B. The watchbirds shocked to kill.

Slaughterhouses in Chicago stopped and cattle starved to death in their pens, because farmers in the Midwest couldn't cut hay or harvest grain.

No one had told the watchbirds that all life depends on carefully balanced murders.

Starvation didn't concern the watchbirds, since it was an act of omission.

Their interest lay only in acts of commission.

Hunters sat home, glaring at the silver dots in the sky, longing to shoot them down. But for the most part, they didn't try. The watchbirds were quick to sense the murder intent and to punish it.

Fishing boats swung idle at their moorings in San Pedro and Gloucester. Fish were living organisms.

Farmers cursed and spat and died, trying to harvest the crop. Grain was alive and thus worthy of protection. Potatoes were as important to the watchbird as any other living organism. The death of a blade of grass was equal to the assassination of a President—

To the watchbirds.

And, of course, certain machines were living. This followed, since the watchbirds were machines and living.

God help you if you maltreated your radio. Turning it off meant killing it. Obviously – its voice was silenced, the red glow of its tubes faded, it grew cold.

The watchbirds tried to guard their other charges. Wolves were slaughtered, trying to kill rabbits. Rabbits were electrocuted, trying to eat vegetables. Creepers were burned out in the act of strangling trees.

A butterfly was executed, caught in the act of outraging a rose.

This control was spasmodic, because of the fewness of the watchbirds. A billion watchbirds couldn't have carried out the ambitious project set by the thousands.

The effect was of a murderous force, ten thousand

bolts of irrational lightning raging around the country, striking a thousand times a day.

Lightning which anticipated your moves and punished your intentions.

'Gentlemen, *please*,' the government representative begged. 'We must hurry.'

The seven manufacturers stopped talking.

'Before we begin this meeting formally,' the president of Monroe said, 'I want to say something. We do not feel ourselves responsible for this unhappy state of affairs. It was a government project; the government must accept the responsibility, both moral and financial.'

Gelsen shrugged his shoulders. It was hard to believe that these men, just a few weeks ago, had been willing to accept the glory of saving the world. Now they wanted to shrug off the responsibility when the salvation went amiss.

'I'm positive that that need not concern us now,' the representative assured him. 'We must hurry. You engineers have done an excellent job. I am proud of the co-operation you have shown in this emergency. You are hereby empowered to put the outlined plan into action.'

'Wait a minute,' Gelsen said.

'There is no time.'

'The plan's no good.'

'Don't you think it will work?'

'Of course it will work. But I'm afraid the cure will be worse than the disease.'

The manufacturers looked as though they would have enjoyed throttling Gelsen. He didn't hesitate.

'Haven't we learned yet?' he asked. 'Don't you see that you can't cure human problems by mechanization?'

'Mr Gelsen,' the president of Monroe said, 'I would enjoy hearing you philosophize, but, unfortunately, people are being killed. Crops are being ruined. There is famine in some sections of the country already. The watchbirds must be stopped at once.'

'Murder must be stopped, too. I remember all of us agreeing upon that. But this is not the way.'

'What would you suggest?' the representative asked.

Gelsen took a deep breath. What he was about to say took all the courage he had.

'Let the watchbirds run down by themselves,' Gelsen suggested.

There was a near-riot. The government representative broke it up.

'Let's take our lesson,' Gelsen urged, 'admit that we were wrong trying to cure human problems by mechanical means. Start again. Use machines, yes, but not as judges and teachers and fathers.'

'Ridiculous,' the representative said coldly. 'Mr Gelsen, you are overwrought. I suggest you control yourself.' He cleared his throat. 'All of you are ordered by the President to carry out the plan you have submitted.' He looked sharply at Gelsen. 'Not to do so will be treason.'

'I'll co-operate to the best of my ability,' Gelsen said.

'Good. Those assembly lines must be rolling within the week.'

Gelsen walked out of the room alone. Now he was confused again. Had he been right or was he just another

133

visionary? Certainly, he hadn't explained himself with much clarity.

Did he know what he meant?

Gelsen cursed under his breath. He wondered why he couldn't ever be sure of anything. Weren't there any values he could hold on to?

He hurried to the airport and to his plant.

The watchbird was operating erratically now. Many of its delicate parts were out of line, worn by almost continuous operation. But gallantly it responded when the stimuli came.

A spider was attacking a fly. The watchbird swooped down to the rescue.

Simultaneously, it became aware of something overhead. The watchbird wheeled to meet it.

There was a sharp crackle and a power bolt whizzed by the watchbird's wing. Angrily, it spat a shock wave.

The attacker was heavily insulated. Again it spat at the watchbird. This time, a bolt smashed through a wing. The watchbird darted away, but the attacker went after it in a burst of speed, throwing out more crackling power.

The watchbird fell, but managed to send out its message. Urgent! A new menace to living organisms and this was the deadliest yet.

Other watchbirds around the country integrated the message. Their thinking centres searched for an answer.

'Well, Chief, they bagged fifty today,' Macintyre said, coming into Gelsen's office.

'Fine,' Gelsen said, not looking at the engineer.

'Not so fine,' Macintyre sat down. 'Lord, I'm tired! It was seventy-two yesterday.'

'I know.' On Gelsen's desk were several dozen lawsuits, which he was sending to the government with a prayer.

'They'll pick up again, though,' Macintyre said confidently. 'The Hawks are especially built to hunt down watchbirds. They're stronger, faster, and they've got better armour. We really rolled them out in a hurry, huh?'

'We sure did.'

'The watchbirds are pretty good, too,' Macintyre had to admit. 'They're learning to take cover. They're trying a lot of stunts. You know, each one that goes down tells the others something.'

Gelsen didn't answer.

'But anything the watchbirds can do, the Hawks can do better,' Macintyre said cheerfully. 'The Hawks have special learning circuits for hunting. They're more flexible than the watchbirds. They learn faster.'

Gelsen gloomily stood up, stretched, and walked to the window. The sky was blank. Looking out, he realized that his uncertainties were over. Right or wrong, he had made up his mind.

'Tell me,' he said, still watching the sky, 'what will the Hawks hunt after they get all the watchbirds?'

'Huh?' Macintyre said. 'Why—'

'Just to be on the safe side, you'd better design something to hunt down the Hawks. Just in case, I mean.'

'You think—'

'All I know is that the Hawks are self-controlled. So were the watchbirds. Remote control would have been too slow, the argument went on. The idea was to get the watchbirds and get them fast. That meant no restricting circuits.'

'We can dope something out,' Macintyre said uncertainly.

'You've got an aggressive machine up in the air now. A murder machine. Before that it was an anti-murder machine. Your next gadget will have to be even more self-sufficient, won't it?'

Macintyre didn't answer.

'I don't hold you responsible,' Gelsen said. 'It's me. It's everyone.'

In the air outside was a swift-moving dot.

'That's what comes,' said Gelsen, 'of giving a machine the job that was our own responsibility.'

Overhead, a Hawk was zeroing in on a watchbird. The armoured murder machine had learned a lot in a few days. Its sole function was to kill. At present it was impelled towards a certain type of living organism, metallic like itself.

But the Hawk had just discovered that there were other types of living organisms, too—

Which had to be murdered.

Warm

Anders lay on his bed, fully dressed except for his shoes and black bow tie, contemplating, with a certain uneasiness, the evening before him. In twenty minutes he would pick up Judy at her apartment, and that was the uneasy part of it.

He had realized, only seconds ago, that he was in love with her.

Well, he'd tell her. The evening would be memorable. He would propose, there would be kisses, and the seal of acceptance would, figuratively speaking, be stamped across his forehead.

Not too pleasant an outlook, he decided. It really would be much more comfortable not to be in love. What had done it? A look, a touch, a thought? It didn't take much, he knew, and stretched his arms for a thorough yawn.

'Help me!' a voice said.

His muscles spasmed, cutting off the yawn in mid-moment. He sat upright on the bed, then grinned and lay back again.

'You must help me,' the voice insisted.

Anders sat up, reached for a polished shoe and fitted it on, giving his full attention to the tying of the laces.

'Can you hear me?' the voice asked. 'You can, can't you?'

That did it. 'Yes, I can hear you,' Anders said, still in a high good humour. 'Don't tell me you're my guilty subconscious, attacking me for a childhood trauma I never bothered to resolve. I suppose you want me to join a monastery.'

'I don't know what you're talking about,' the voice said. 'I'm no one's subconscious. I'm *me*. Will you help me?'

Anders believed in voices as much as anyone; that is, he didn't believe in them at all, until he heard them. Swiftly he catalogued the possibilities. Schizophrenia was the best answer, of course, and one in which his colleagues would concur. But Anders had a lamentable confidence in his own sanity. In which case—

'Who are you?' he asked.

'I don't know,' the voice answered.

Anders realized that the voice was speaking within his own mind. Very suspicious.

'You don't know who you are,' Anders stated. 'Very well. *Where* are you?'

'I don't know that, either.' The voice paused, and went on. 'Look, I know how ridiculous this must sound. Believe me, I'm in some sort of limbo. I don't know how I got here or who I am, but I want desperately to get out. Will you help me?'

Still fighting the idea of a voice speaking within his head, Anders knew that his next decision was vital. He had to accept – or reject – his own sanity.

He accepted it.

'All right,' Anders said, lacing the other shoe. 'I'll grant that you're a person in trouble, and that you're in some sort of telepathic contact with me. Is there anything else you can tell me?'

'I'm afraid not,' the voice said, with infinite sadness. 'You'll have to find out for yourself.'

'Can you contact anyone else?'

'No.'

'Then how can you talk with me?'

'I don't know.'

Anders walked to his bureau mirror and adjusted his black bow tie, whistling softly under his breath. Having just discovered that he was in love, he wasn't going to let a little thing like a voice in his mind disturb him.

'I really don't see how I can be of any help,' Anders said, brushing a bit of lint from his jacket. 'You don't know where you are, and there don't seem to be any distinguishing landmarks. How am I to find you?' He turned and looked around the room to see if he had forgotten anything.

'I'll know when you're close,' the voice said. 'You were warm just then.'

'Just then?' All he had done was look around the room. He did so again, turning his head slowly. Then it happened.

The room, from one angle, looked different. It was suddenly a mixture of muddled colours, instead of the carefully blended pastel shades he had selected.

The lines of wall, floor and ceiling were strangely off proportion, zigzag, unrelated.

Then everything went back to normal.

'You were *very* warm,' the voice said.

Anders resisted the urge to scratch his head, for fear

of disarranging his carefully combed hair. What he had seen wasn't so strange. Everyone sees one or two things in his life that make him doubt his normality, doubt his sanity, doubt his very existence. For a moment the orderly Universe is disarranged and the fabric of belief is ripped.

But the moment passes.

Anders remembered once, as a boy, awakening in his room in the middle of the night. How strange everything had looked! Chairs, table, all out of proportion, swollen in the dark. The ceiling pressing down, as in a dream.

But that also had passed.

'Well, old man,' he said, 'if I get warm again, tell me!'

'I will,' the voice in his head whispered. 'I'm sure you'll find me.'

'I'm glad you're so sure,' Anders said gaily, switched off the lights and left.

Lovely and smiling, Judy greeted him at the door. Looking at her, Anders sensed her knowledge of the moment. Had she felt the change in him, or predicted it? Or was love making him grin like an idiot?

'Would you like a before-party drink?' she asked.

He nodded, and she led him across the room, to the improbable green-and-yellow couch. Sitting down, Anders decided he would tell her when she came back with the drink. No use in putting off the fatal moment. A lemming in love, he told himself.

'You're getting warm again,' the voice said.

He had almost forgotten his invisible friend. Or fiend, as the case could well be. What would Judy say if she knew he was hearing voices? Little things like that, he reminded himself, often break up the best of romances.

'Here!' she said, handing him a drink.

Still smiling, he noticed. The number two smile – to a prospective suitor, provocative and understanding. It had been preceded, in their relationship, by the number one nice-girl smile, the don't-misunderstand-me smile, to be worn on all occasions, until the correct words have been mumbled.

'That's right,' the voice said. 'It's in how you look at things.'

Look at what? Anders glanced at Judy, annoyed at his thoughts. If he was going to play the lover, let him play it. Even through the astigmatic haze of love, he was able to appreciate her blue-grey eyes, her fine skin (if one over-looked a tiny blemish on the left temple), her lips, slightly reshaped by lipstick.

'How did your classes go to-day?' she asked.

Well, of course she'd ask that, Anders thought. Love is marking time.

'All right,' he said. 'Teaching psychology to young apes—'

'Oh, come now!'

'Warmer,' the voice said.

What's the matter with me, Anders wondered. She really is a lovely girl. The *gestalt* that is Judy, a pattern of thoughts, expressions, movements, making up the girl I—

I what?

Love?

Anders shifted his long body uncertainly on the couch. He didn't quite understand how this train of thought had begun. It annoyed him. The analytical young instructor was better off in the classroom. Couldn't science wait until 9.10 in the morning?

'I was thinking about you to-day,' Judy said, and Anders knew that she had sensed the change in his mood.

'Do you see?' the voice asked him. 'You're getting much better at it.'

'I don't see anything,' Anders thought, but the voice was right. It was as though he had a clear line of inspection into Judy's mind. Her feelings were nakedly apparent to him, as meaningless as his room had been in that flash of undistorted thought.

'I really was thinking about you,' she repeated.

'Now look!' the voice said.

Anders, watching the expressions on Judy's face, felt the strangeness descend on him. He was back in the nightmare perception of that moment in his room. This time it was as though he were watching a machine in a laboratory. The object of this operation was the evocation and preservation of a particular mood. The machine goes through a searching process, invoking trains of ideas to achieve the desired end.

'Oh, were you?' he asked, amazed at his new perspective.

'Yes – I wondered what you were doing at noon,' the reactive machine opposite him on the couch said, expanding its shapely chest slightly.

'Good,' the voice said, commending him for his perception.

'Dreaming of you, of course,' he said to the flesh-clad skeleton behind the total *gestalt* Judy. The flesh machine rearranged its limbs, widened its mouth to denote pleasure. The mechanism searched through a complex of fears, hopes, worries, through half-remembrances of analogous situations, analogous solutions.

And this was what he loved. Anders saw too clearly and hated himself for seeing. Through his new nightmare perception, the absurdity of the entire room struck him.

'Were you really?' the articulating skeleton asked him.

'You're coming closer,' the voice whispered.

To what? The personality? There was no such thing. There was no true cohesion, no depth, nothing except a web of surface reactions, stretched across automatic visceral movements.

He was coming closer to the truth.

'Sure,' he said sourly.

The machine stirred, searching for a response.

Anders felt a quick tremor of fear at the sheer alien quality of his viewpoint. His sense of formalism had been sloughed off, his agreed-upon reactions by-passed. What would be revealed next?

He was seeing clearly, he realized, as perhaps no man had ever seen before. It was an oddly exhilarating thought.

But could he still return to normality?

'Can I get you a drink?' the reaction machine asked.

At that moment Anders was as thoroughly out of love as man could be. Viewing one's intended as a depersonalized, sexless piece of machinery is not especially conducive to love. But it is quite stimulating, intellectually.

Anders didn't want normality. A curtain was being raised and he wanted to see behind it. What was it some Russian scientist – Ouspensky, wasn't it – had said?

143

'*Think in other categories.*'

That was what he was doing, and would continue to do.

'Good-bye,' he said suddenly.

The machine watched him, open-mouthed, as he walked out the door. Delayed circuit reactions kept it silent until it heard the lift door close.

'You were very warm in there,' the voice within his head whispered, once he was on the street. 'But you still don't understand everything.'

'Tell me, then!' Anders said, marvelling a little at his equanimity. In an hour he had bridged the gap to a completely different viewpoint, yet it seemed perfectly natural.

'I can't,' the voice said. 'You must find it yourself.'

'Well, let's see now,' Anders began. He looked around at the masses of masonry, the convention of streets cutting through the architectural piles. 'Human life,' he said, 'is a series of conventions. When you look at a girl, you're supposed to see – a pattern, not the underlying formlessness.'

'That's true,' the voice agreed, but with a shade of doubt.

'Basically, there is no form. Man produces *gestalts*, and cuts form out of the plethora of nothingness. It's like looking at a set of lines and saying that they represent a figure. We look at a mass of material, extract it from the background and say it's a man. But in truth, there is no such thing. There are only the humanizing features that we – myopically – attach to it. Matter is conjoined, a matter of viewpoint.'

'You're not seeing it now,' said the voice.

'Damn it,' Anders said. He was certain that he was on the track of something big, perhaps something ultimate. 'Everyone's had the experience. At some time in his life, everyone looks at a familiar object and can't make any sense out of it. Momentarily, the *gestalt* fails, but the true moment of sight passes. The mind reverts to the super-imposed pattern. Normalcy continues.'

The voice was silent. Anders walked on, through the *gestalt* city.

'There's something else, isn't there?' Anders asked.

'Yes.'

What could that be, he asked himself. Through clearing eyes, Anders looked at the formality he had called his world.

He wondered momentarily if he would have come to this if the voice hadn't guided him. Yes, he decided after a few moments, it was inevitable.

But who was the voice? And what had he left out?

'Let's see what a party looks like now!' he said to the voice.

The party was a masquerade; the guests were all wearing their faces. To Anders, their motives, individually and collectively, were painfully apparent. Then his vision began to clear further.

He saw that the people weren't truly individual. They were discontinuous lumps of flesh sharing a common vocabulary, yet not even truly discontinuous.

The lumps of flesh were a part of the decoration of the room and almost indistinguishable from it. They were one with the lights, which lent their tiny vision. They were joined to the sounds they made, a few feeble tones out of the great possibility of sound. They blended into the walls.

The kaleidoscopic view came so fast that Anders had trouble sorting his new impressions. He knew now that these people existed only as patterns, on the same basis as the sounds they made and the things they thought they saw.

Gestalts, sifted out of the vast, unbearable real world.

'Where's Judy?' a discontinuous lump of flesh asked him. This particular lump possessed enough nervous mannerisms to convince the other lumps of his reality. He wore a loud tie as further evidence.

'She's sick,' Anders said. The flesh quivered into an instant sympathy. Lines of formal mirth shifted to formal woe.

'Hope it isn't anything serious,' the vocal flesh remarked.

'You're warmer,' the voice said to Anders.

Anders looked at the object in front of him.

'She hasn't long to live,' he stated.

The flesh quivered. Stomach and intestines contracted in sympathetic fear. Eyes distended, mouth quivered.

The loud tie remained the same.

'My God! you don't mean it?'

'What are you?' Anders asked quietly.

'What do you mean?' the indignant flesh attached to the tie demanded. Serene within its reality, it gaped at Anders. Its mouth twitched, undeniable proof that it was real and sufficient. 'You're drunk,' it sneered.

Anders laughed and left the party.

'There is still something you don't know,' the voice said. 'But you were hot. I could feel you near me.'

'What are you?' Anders asked again.

'I don't know,' the voice admitted. 'I am a person. I am I. I am trapped.'

'So are we all,' Anders said. He walked on asphalt, surrounded by heaps of concrete, silicates, aluminium and iron alloys. Shapeless, meaningless heaps that made up the *gestalt* city.

And then there were the imaginary lines of demarcation dividing city from city, the artificial boundaries of water and land.

All ridiculous.

'Give me a dime for some coffee, mister?' something asked, a thing indistinguishable from any other thing.

'Old Bishop Berkeley would give a non-existent dime to your non-existent presence,' Anders said gaily.

'I'm really in a bad way,' the voice whined, and Anders perceived that it was no more than a series of modulated vibrations.

'Yes! Go on!' the voice commanded.

'If you could spare me a quarter—' the vibrations said, with a deep pretence at meaning.

No, what was there behind the senseless patterns? Flesh, mass. What was that? All made up of atoms.

'I'm really hungry,' the intricately arranged atoms muttered.

All atoms. Conjoined. There were no true separations between atom and atom. Flesh was stone, stone was light. Anders looked at the masses of atoms that were pretending to solidity, meaning and reason.

'Can't you help me?' a clump of atoms asked. But the clump was identical with all the other atoms. Once you ignored the superimposed patterns, you could see the atoms were random, scattered.

'I don't believe in you,' Anders said.

The pile of atoms was gone.

'Yes!' the voice cried. 'Yes!'

'I don't believe in any of it,' Anders said. After all, what was an atom?'

'Go on!' the voice shouted. 'You're hot. Go on!'

What was an atom? An empty space surrounded by an empty space.

Absurd!

'Then it's all false,' Anders said. And he was alone under the stars.

'That's right,' the voice within his head screamed. 'Nothing!'

But stars, Anders thought. How can one believe—

The stars disappeared. Anders was in a grey nothingness, a void. There was nothing around him except shapeless grey.

Where was the voice?

Gone.

Anders perceived the delusion behind the greyness, and then there was nothing at all.

Complete nothingness, and himself within it.

Where was he? What did it mean? Anders' mind tried to add it up.

Impossible. *That* couldn't be true.

Again the score was tabulated, but Anders' mind couldn't accept the total. In desperation, the overloaded mind erased the figures, eradicated the knowledge, erased itself.

'Where am I?'

In nothingness. Alone.

Trapped.

'Who am I?'

A voice.

The voice of Anders searched the nothingness, shouted, 'Is there anyone here?'

No answer.

But there was someone. All directions were the same, yet moving along one he could make contact – with someone. The voice of Anders reached back to someone who could save him, perhaps.

'Save me!' the voice said to Anders, lying fully dressed on his bed, except for his shoes and black bow tie.

Specialist

The photon storm struck without warning, pouncing upon the Ship from behind a bank of giant red stars. Eye barely had time to flash a last-second warning through Talker before it was upon them.

It was Talker's third journey into deep space, and his first light-pressure storm. He felt a sudden pang of fear as the Ship yawed violently, caught the force of the wave-front and careened end for end. Then the fear was gone, replaced by a strong pulse of excitement.

Why should he be afraid, he asked himself – hadn't he been trained for just this sort of emergency?

He had been talking to Feeder when the storm hit, but he cut off the conversation abruptly. He hoped Feeder would be all right. It was the youngster's first deep-space trip.

The wire-like filaments that made up most of Talker's body were extended throughout the Ship. Quickly he withdrew all except the ones linking him to Eye, Engine, and the Walls. This was strictly their job now. The rest of the Crew would have to shift for themselves until the storm was over.

Eye had flattened his disc-like body against a Wall, and had one seeing organ extended outside the Ship. For greater concentration, the rest of his seeing organs were collapsed, clustered against his body.

Through Eye's seeing organ, Talker watched the storm. He translated Eye's purely visual image into a direction for Engine, who shoved the Ship around to meet the waves. At appreciably the same time, Talker translated direction into velocity for the Walls who stiffened to meet the shocks.

The co-ordination was swift and sure – Eye measuring the waves, Talker relaying the messages to Engine and Walls, Engine driving the Ship nose-first into the waves, and Walls bracing to meet the shock.

Talker forgot any fear he might have had in the swiftly functioning teamwork. He had no time to think. As the Ship's communication system, he had to translate and flash his messages at top speed, co-ordinating information and directing action.

In a matter of minutes, the storm was over.

'All right,' Talker said. 'Let's see if there was any damage!' His filaments had become tangled during the storm, but he untwisted and extended them through the Ship, plugging everyone into the circuit. 'Engine?'

'I'm fine,' Engine said. The tremendous old fellow had dampened his plates during the storm, easing down the atomic explosions in his stomach. No storm could catch an experienced spacer like Engine unaware.

'Walls?'

The Walls reported one by one, and this took a long time. There were almost a thousand of them, thin, rectangular fellows making up the entire skin of the Ship. Naturally, they had reinforced their edges during the storm, giving the whole Ship resiliency. But one or two were dented badly.

Doctor announced that he was all right. He removed Talker's filament from his head, taking himself out of circuit, and went to work on the dented Walls. Made mostly of hands, Doctor had clung to an Accumulator during the storm.

'Let's go a little faster now!' Talker said, remembering that there still was the problem of determining where they were. He opened the circuit to the four Accumulators. 'How are you?' he asked.

There was no answer. The Accumulators were asleep. They had had their receptors open during the storm and were bloated on energy. Talker twitched his filaments around them, but they didn't stir.

'Let me!' Feeder said. Feeder had taken quite a beating before planting his suction cups to a Wall, but his cockiness was intact. He was the only member of the Crew who never needed Doctor's attention; his body was quite capable of repairing itself.

He scuttled across the floor on a dozen or so tentacles, and booted the nearest Accumulator. The big, conial storage unit opened one eye, then closed it again. Feeder kicked him again, getting no response. He reached for the Accumulator's safety valve and drained off some energy.

'Stop that!' the Accumulator said.

'Then wake up and report!' Talker told him.

The Accumulators said testily that they were all right, as any fool could see. They had been anchored to the floor during the storm.

The rest of the inspection went quickly. Thinker was fine, and Eye was ecstatic over the beauty of the storm. There was only one casualty.

Pusher was dead. Bipedal, he didn't have the stability of the rest of the Crew. The storm had caught him in the middle of a floor, thrown him against a stiffened Wall, and broken several of his important bones. He was beyond Doctor's skill to repair.

They were silent for a while. It was always serious when a part of the Ship died. The Ship was a co-operative unit, composed entirely of the Crew. The loss of any member was a blow to all the rest.

It was especially serious now. They had just delivered a cargo to a port several thousand light-years from Galactic Centre. There was no telling where they might be.

Eye crawled to a Wall and extended a seeing organ outside. The Walls let it through, then sealed around it. Eye's organ pushed out, far enough from the Ship so he could view the entire sphere of stars. The picture travelled through Talker, who gave it to Thinker.

Thinker lay in one corner of the room, a great shapeless blob of protoplasm. Within him were all the memories of his space-going ancestors. He considered the picture, compared it rapidly with others stored in his cells, and said, 'No galactic planets within reach.'

Talker automatically translated for everyone. It was what they had feared.

Eye, with Thinker's help, calculated that they were several hundred light-years off their course, on the galactic periphery.

Every Crew member knew what that meant. Without a Pusher to boost the Ship to a multiple of the speed of light, they would never get home. The trip back, without a Pusher, would take longer than most of their lifetimes.

153

'What would you suggest?' Talker asked Thinker.

This was too vague a question for the literal-minded Thinker. He asked to have it rephrased.

'What would be our best line of action,' Talker asked, 'to get back to a galactic planet?'

Thinker needed several minutes to go through all the possibilities stored in his cells. In the meantime, Doctor had patched the Walls and was asking to be given something to eat.

'In a little while we'll all eat,' Talker said, twitching his tendrils nervously. Even though he was the second youngest Crew member – only Feeder was younger – the responsibility was largely on him. This was still an emergency; he had to co-ordinate information and direct action.

One of the Walls suggested that they get good and drunk. This unrealistic solution was vetoed at once. It was typical of the Walls' attitude, however. They were fine workers and good shipmates, but happy-go-lucky fellows at best. When they returned to their home planets, they would probably blow all their wages on a spree.

'Loss of the Ship's Pusher cripples the Ship for sustained faster-than-light speeds,' Thinker began without preamble. 'The nearest galactic planet is four hundred and five light-years off.'

Talker translated all this instantly along his wave-packet body.

'Two courses of action are open. First, the Ship can proceed to the nearest galactic planet under atomic power from Engine. This will take approximately two hundred years. Engine might still be alive at this time, although no one else will.

'Second, locate a primitive planet in this region, upon which are latent Pushers. Find one and train him. Have him push the Ship back to galactic territory.'

Thinker was silent, having given all the possibilities he could find in the memories of his ancestors.

They held a quick vote and decided upon Thinker's second alternative. There was no choice, really. It was the only one which offered them any hope of getting back to their homes.

'All right,' Talker said. 'Let's eat! I think we all deserve it.'

The body of the dead Pusher was shoved into the mouth of Engine, who consumed it at once, breaking down the atoms to energy. Engine was the only member of the Crew who lived on atomic energy.

For the rest, Feeder dashed up and loaded himself from the nearest Accumulator. Then he transformed the food within him into the substances each member ate. His body chemistry changed, altered, adapted, making the different foods for the Crew.

Eye lived entirely on a complex chlorophyll chain. Feeder reproduced this for him, then went over to give Talker his hydrocarbons, and the Walls their chlorine compound. For Doctor he made a facsimile of a silicate fruit that grew on Doctor's native planet.

Finally, feeding was over and the Ship back in order. The Accumulators were stacked in a corner, blissfully sleeping again. Eye was extending his vision as far as he could, shaping his main seeing organ for high-powered telescopic reception. Even in this emergency, Eye couldn't resist making verses. He announced that he was at work on a new narrative poem, called *Peripheral Glow*. No one wanted to hear it, so Eye fed it to Thinker, who stored everything, good or bad, right or wrong.

Engine never slept. Filled to the brim on Pusher, he shoved the Ship along at several times the speed of light.

The Walls were arguing among themselves about who had been the drunkest during their last leave.

Talker decided to make himself comfortable. He released his hold on the Walls and swung in the air, his small round body suspended by his crisscrossed network of filaments.

He thought briefly about Pusher. It was strange. Pusher had been everyone's friend and now he was forgotten. That wasn't because of indifference; it was because the Ship was a unit. The loss of a member was regretted, but the important thing was for the unit to go on.

The Ship raced through the suns of the periphery.

Thinker laid out a search spiral, calculating their odds on finding a Pusher planet at roughly four to one. In a week they found a planet of primitive Walls. Dropping low, they could see the leathery, rectangular fellows basking in the sun, crawling over rocks, stretching themselves thin in order to float in the breeze.

All the Ship's Walls heaved a sigh of nostalgia. It was just like home.

These Walls on the planet hadn't been contacted by a galactic team yet, and were still unaware of their great destiny – to join in the vast Co-operation of the Galaxy.

There were plenty of dead worlds in the spiral, and worlds too young to bear life. They found a planet of

Talkers. The Talkers had extended their spidery communication lines across half a continent.

Talker looked at them eagerly, through Eye. A wave of self-pity washed over him. He remembered home, his family, his friends. He thought of the tree he was going to buy when he got back.

For a moment, Talker wondered what he was doing here, part of a Ship in a far corner of the Galaxy.

He shrugged off the mood. They were bound to find a Pusher planet, if they looked long enough.

At least, he hoped so.

There was a long stretch of arid worlds as the Ship sped through the unexplored periphery. Then a planetful of primeval Engines, swimming in a radio-active ocean.

'This is rich territory,' Feeder said to Talker. 'Galactic should send a Contact party here.'

'They probably will, after we get back,' Talker said.

They were good friends, above and beyond the all-enveloping friendship of the Crew. It wasn't only because they were the youngest Crew members, although that had something to do with it. They both had the same kind of functions and that made for a certain rapport. Talker translated languages; Feeder transformed foods. Also, they looked somewhat alike. Talker was a central core with radiating filaments; Feeder was a central core with radiating tentacles.

Talker thought that Feeder was the next most aware being on the Ship. He was never really able to understand how some of the others carried on the processes of consciousness.

More suns, more planets! Engine started to overheat. Usually, Engine was used only for taking off and landing, and for fine manoeuvring in a planetary group. Now he had been running continuously for weeks, both over and under the speed of light. The strain was telling on him.

Feeder, with Doctor's help, rigged a cooling system for him. It was crude, but it had to suffice. Feeder rearranged nitrogen, oxygen and hydrogen atoms to make a coolant for the system. Doctor diagnosed a long rest for Engine. He said that the gallant old fellow couldn't stand the strain for more than a week.

The search continued, with the Crew's spirits gradually dropping. They all realized that Pushers were rather rare in the Galaxy, as compared to the fertile Walls and Engines.

The Walls were getting pock-marked from interstellar dust. They complained that they would need a full beauty treatment when they got home. Talker assured them that the company would pay for it.

Even Eye was getting bloodshot from staring into space so continuously.

They dipped over another planet. Its characteristics were flashed to Thinker, who mulled over them.

Closer, and they could make out the forms.

Pushers! Primitive Pushers!

They zoomed back into space to make plans. Feeder produced twenty-three different kinds of intoxicants for a celebration.

The Ship wasn't fit to function for three days.

'Everyone ready now?' Talker asked, a bit fuzzily. He had a hangover that burned all along his nerve ends. What a drunk he had thrown! He had a vague recollection of embracing Engine, and inviting him to share his tree when they got home.

He shuddered at the idea.

The rest of the Crew were pretty shaky, too. The Walls were letting air leak into space; they were just too wobbly to seal their edges properly. Doctor had passed out.

But the worst off was Feeder. Since his system could adapt to any type of fuel except atomic, he had been sampling every batch he made, whether it was an unbalanced iodine, pure oxygen or a supercharged ester. He was really miserable. His tentacles, usually a healthy aqua, were shot through with orange streaks. His system was working furiously, purging itself of everything, and Feeder was suffering the effects of the purge.

The only sober ones were Thinker and Engine. Thinker didn't drink, which was unusual for a spacer, though typical of Thinker, and Engine couldn't.

They listened while Thinker reeled off some astounding facts. From Eye's pictures of the planet's surface, Thinker had detected the presence of metallic construction. He put forth the alarming suggestion that these Pushers had constructed a mechanical civilization.

'That's impossible,' three of the Walls said flatly, and most of the Crew were inclined to agree with them. All the metal they had ever seen had been buried in the ground or lying around in worthless oxidized chunks.

'Do you mean that they make things out of metal?' Talker demanded. 'Out of just plain dead metal? What could they make?'

'They couldn't make anything,' Feeder said positively.

'It would break down constantly. I mean metal doesn't *know* when it's weakening.'

But it seemed to be true. Eye magnified his pictures, and everyone could see that the Pushers had made vast shelters, vehicles, and other articles from inanimate material.

The reason for this was not readily apparent, but it wasn't a good sign. However, the really hard part was over. The Pusher planet had been found. All that remained was the relatively easy job of convincing a native Pusher.

That shouldn't be too difficult. Talker knew that cooperation was the keystone of the Galaxy, even among primitive peoples.

The Crew decided not to land in a populated region. Of course, there was no reason not to expect a friendly greeting, but it was the job of a Contact Team to get in touch with them as a race. All they wanted was an individual.

Accordingly, they picked out a sparsely populated landmass, drifting in while that side of the planet was dark.

They were able to locate a solitary Pusher almost at once.

Eye adapted his vision to see in the dark, and they followed the Pusher's movements. He lay down, after a while, beside a small fire. Thinker told them that his was a well-known resting habit of Pushers.

Just before dawn, the Walls opened, and Feeder, Talker and Doctor came out.

Feeder dashed forward and tapped the creature on the shoulder. Talker followed with a communication tendril.

The Pusher opened his seeing organs, blinked them,

and made a movement with his eating organ. Then he leaped to his feet and started to run.

The three Crew members were amazed. The Pusher hadn't even waited to find out what the three of them wanted!

Talker extended a filament rapidly, and caught the Pusher, fifty feet away, by a limb. The Pusher fell.

'Treat him gently!' Feeder said. 'He might be startled by our appearance. He twitched his tendrils at the idea of a Pusher – one of the strangest sights in the Galaxy, with his multiple organs – being startled at someone else's appearance.

Feeder and Doctor scurried to the fallen Pusher, picked him up and carried him back to the Ship.

The Walls sealed again. They released the Pusher and prepared to talk.

As soon as he was free, the Pusher sprang to his limbs and ran at the place where the Walls had sealed. He pounded against them frantically, his eating organ open and vibrating.

'Stop that!' the Wall said. He bulged, and the Pusher tumbled to the floor. Instantly, he jumped up and started to run forward.

'Stop him!' Talker said. 'He might hurt himself.'

One of the Accumulators woke up enough to roll into the Pusher's path. The Pusher fell, got up again, and ran on.

Talker had his filaments in the front of the Ship also, and he caught the Pusher in the bow. The Pusher started to tear at his tendrils, and Talker let go hastily.

'Plug him into the communication system!' Feeder shouted. 'Maybe we can reason with him.'

Talker advanced a filament towards the Pusher's head, waving it in the universal sign of communication. But the Pusher continued his amazing behaviour, jumping out of the way. He had a piece of metal in his hand and he was waving it frantically.

'What do you think he's going to do with that?' Feeder asked. The Pusher started to attack the side of the Ship, pounding at one of the Walls. The Wall stiffened instinctively and the metal snapped.

'Leave him alone,' Talker said. 'Give him a chance to calm down.'

Talker consulted with Thinker, but they couldn't decide what to do about the Pusher. He wouldn't accept communication. Every time Talker extended a filament, the Pusher showed all the signs of violent panic. Temporarily, it was an impasse.

Thinker vetoed the plan of finding another Pusher on the planet. He considered this Pusher's behaviour typical; nothing would be gained by approaching another. Also, a planet was supposed to be contacted only by a Contact Team.

If they couldn't communicate with this Pusher, they never would with another on the planet.

'I think I know what the trouble is,' Eye said. He crawled up on an Accumulator. 'These Pushers have evolved a mechanical civilization. Consider for a minute how they went about it. They developed the use of their fingers, like Doctor, to shape metal. They utilized their seeing organs, like myself. And probably countless other organs.' He paused for effect.

'These Pushers have become unspecialized.'

They argued over it for several hours. The Walls maintained that no intelligent creature could be unspecialized. It was unknown in the Galaxy. But the evidence was before them – The Pusher cities, their vehicles— This Pusher, exemplifying the rest, seemed capable of a multitude of things.

He was able to do everything except Push.

Thinker supplied a partial explanation. 'This is not a primitive planet. It is relatively old and should have been in the Co-operation thousands of years ago. Since it was not, the Pushers upon it were robbed of their birthright. Their ability, their speciality, was to Push, but there was nothing *to* Push. Naturally, they have developed a deviant culture.

'Exactly what this culture is, we can only guess. But on the basis of the evidence, there is reason to believe that these Pushers are – un-co-operative.'

Thinker had a habit of uttering the most shattering statement in the quietest possible way.

'It is entirely possible,' Thinker went on inexorably, 'that these Pushers will have nothing to do with us. In which case, our chances are approximately two hundred and eighty-three to one against finding another Pusher planet.'

We can't be sure he won't co-operate,' Talker said, 'until we get him into communication.' He found it almost impossible to believe that any intelligent creature would refuse to co-operate willingly.

'But how?' Feeder asked. They decided upon a course of action. Doctor walked slowly up to the Pusher, who backed away from him. In the meantime, Talker extended a filament outside the Ship, around, and in again, behind the Pusher.

The Pusher backed against a Wall – and Talker shoved the filament through the Pusher's head, into the communication socket in the centre of his brain.

The Pusher collapsed.

When he came to, Feeder and Doctor had to hold the Pusher's limbs, or he would have ripped out the communication line. Talker exercised his skill in learning the Pusher's language.

It wasn't too hard. All Pusher languages were of the same family, and this was no exception. Talker was able to catch enough surface thoughts to form a pattern.

He tried to communicate with the Pusher.

The Pusher was silent.

'I think he needs food,' Feeder said. They remembered that it had been almost two days since they had taken the Pusher on board. Feeder worked up some standard Pusher food and offered it.

'My God! A steak!' the Pusher said.

The Crew cheered along Talker's communication circuits. The Pusher had said his first words.

Talker examined the words and searched his memory. He knew about two hundred Pusher languages and many more simple variations. He found that this Pusher was speaking a cross between two Pusher tongues.

After the Pusher had eaten, he looked around. Talker caught his thoughts and broadcast them to the Crew.

The Pusher had a queer way of looking at the Ship. He saw it as a riot of colours. The walls undulated. In front of him was something resembling a gigantic spider, coloured black and green, with his web running all over the Ship and into the heads of all the creatures. He saw Eye as a strange, naked little animal, something between a skinned rabbit and an egg yolk – whatever those things were.

Talker was fascinated by the new perspective the Pusher's mind gave him. He had never seen things that way before. But now that the Pusher was pointing it out, Eye *was* a pretty funny-looking creature.

They settled down to communication.

'What in hell *are* you things?' the Pusher asked, much calmer now than he had been during the two days. 'Why did you grab me? Have I gone nuts?'

'No,' Talker said, 'you are not psychotic. We are a galactic trading ship. We were blown off our course by a storm and our Pusher was killed.'

'Well, what does that have to do with me?'

'We would like you to join our crew,' Talker said, 'to be our new Pusher.'

The Pusher thought it over after the situation was explained to him. Talker could catch the feeling of conflict in the Pusher's thoughts. He hadn't decided whether to accept this as a real situation or not. Finally, the Pusher decided that he wasn't crazy.

'Look, boys,' he said, 'I don't know what you are or how this makes sense. I have to get out of here. I'm on a furlough, and if I don't get back soon, the U.S. Army's going to be very interested.'

Talker asked the Pusher to give him more information about 'army', and he fed it to Thinker.

'These Pushers engage in personal combat,' was Thinker's conclusion.

'But *why?*' Talker asked. Sadly he admitted to himself that Thinker might have been right; the Pusher didn't show many signs of willingness to co-operate.

'I'd like to help you lads out,' Pusher said, 'but I don't know where you get the idea that I could push anything this size. You'd need a whole division of tanks just to budge it.'

'Do you approve of these wars?' Talker asked, getting a suggestion from Thinker.

'Nobody likes war – not those who have to do the dying at least.'

'Then why do you fight them?'

The Pusher made a gesture with his eating organ, which Eye picked up and sent to Thinker. 'It's kill or be killed. You guys know what war is, don't you?'

'We don't have any wars,' Talker said.

'You're lucky,' the Pusher said bitterly. 'We do. Plenty of them.'

'Of course,' Talker said. He had the full explanation from Thinker now. 'Would you like to end them?'

'Of course I would.'

'Then come with us! Be our Pusher!'

The Pusher stood up and walked up to an Accumulator. He sat down on it and doubled the ends of his upper limbs.

'How the hell can I stop all wars?' the Pusher demanded. 'Even if I went to the big shots and told them—'

'You won't have to,' Talker said. 'All you have to do is come with us. Push us to our base. Galactic will send a Contact Team to your planet. That will end your wars.'

'The hell you say,' the Pusher replied. 'You boys are stranded here, huh? Good enough! No monsters are going to take over Earth.'

Bewildered, Talker tried to understand the reasoning. Had he said something wrong? Was it possible that the Pusher didn't understand him?

'I thought you wanted to end wars,' Talker said.

'Sure I do. But I don't want anyone *making* us stop. I'm no traitor. I'd rather fight.'

'No one will make you stop. You will just stop because there will be no further need for fighting.'

'Do you know why we're fighting?'

'It's obvious.'

'Yeah? What's your explanation?'

'You Pushers have been separated from the main-stream of the Galaxy,' Talker explained. 'You have your speciality – pushing – but nothing to push. Accordingly, you have no real jobs. You play with things – metal, in-animate objects – but find no real satisfaction. Robbed of your true vocation, you fight from sheer frustration.

'Once you find your place in the galactic Co-opera-tion – and I assure you that it is an important place – your fighting will stop. Why should you fight, which is an unnatural occupation, when you can push? Also, your mechanical civilization will end, since there will be no need for it.'

The Pusher shook his head in what Talker guessed was a gesture of confusion. 'What is this pushing?'

Talker told him as well as he could. Since the job was out of his scope, he had only a general idea of what a Pusher did.

'You mean to say that *that* is what every Earthman should be doing?'

'Of course,' Talker said. 'It is your great speciality.'

The Pusher thought about it for several minutes. 'I think you want a physicist or a mentalist or something. I could never do anything like that. I'm a junior architect. And besides – well, it's difficult to explain.'

But Talker had already caught Pusher's objection. He saw a Pusher female in his thoughts. No, two, three. And he caught a feeling of loneliness, strangeness. The Pusher was filled with doubts. He was afraid.

'When we reach galactic,' Talker said, hoping it was the right thing, 'you can meet other Pushers. Pusher females, too. All you Pushers look alike, so you should become friends with them. As far as loneliness in the Ship goes – it just doesn't exist. You don't understand the Co-operation yet. No one is lonely in the Co-operation.'

The Pusher was still considering the idea of there being other Pushers. Talker couldn't understand why he was so startled at that. The Galaxy was filled with Pushers, Feeders, Talkers, and many other species, endlessly duplicated.

'I can't believe that anybody could end all war,' Pusher said. 'How do I know you're not lying?'

Talker felt as if he had been struck in the core. Thinker must have been right when he said these Pushers would be un-co-operative. Was this going to be the end of Talker's career? Were he and the rest of the Crew going to spend the rest of their lives in space, because of the stupidity of a bunch of Pushers?

Even thinking this, Talker was able to feel sorry for

the Pusher. It must be terrible, he thought. Doubting, uncertain, never trusting anyone. If these Pushers didn't find their place in the Galaxy, they would exterminate themselves. Their place in the Co-operation was long overdue.

'What can I do to convince you?' Talker asked.

In despair, he opened all the circuits to the Pusher. He let the Pusher see Engine's good-natured gruffness, the devil-may-care humour of the Walls; he showed him Eye's poetic attempts, and Feeder's cocky good nature. He opened his own mind and showed the Pusher a picture of his home planet, his family, the tree he was planning to buy when he got home.

The pictures told the story of all of them, from different planets, representing different ethics, united by a common bond – the galactic Co-operation.

The Pusher watched it all in silence.

After a while, he shook his head. The thought accompanying the gesture was uncertain, weak – but negative.

Talker told the Walls to open. They did, and the Pusher stared in amazement.

'You may leave,' Talker said. 'Just remove the communication line and go.'

'What will you do?'

'We will look for another Pusher planet.'

'Where? Mars? Venus?'

'We don't know. All we can do is hope there is another in this region.'

The Pusher looked at the opening, then back at the Crew. He hesitated and his face screwed up in a grimace of indecision.

'All that you showed me was true?'

No answer was necessary.

'All right,' the Pusher said suddenly. 'I'll go. I'm a damned fool, but I'll go. If this means what you say – it *must* mean what you say!'

Talker saw that the agony of the Pusher's decision had forced him out of contact with reality. He believed that he was in a dream, where decisions are easy and unimportant.

'There's just one little trouble,' Pusher said with the lightness of hysteria. 'Boys, I'll be damned if I know how to push. You said something about faster-than-light? I can't even run the mile in an hour.'

'Of course you can push,' Talker assured him, hoping he was right. He knew what a Pusher's abilities were; but this one—

'Just try it.'

'Sure,' Pusher agreed. 'I'll probably wake up out of this, anyhow.'

They sealed the ship for take-off while Pusher talked to himself.

'Funny,' Pusher said. 'I thought a camping trip would be a nice way to spend a furlough and all I do is get nightmares!'

Engine boosted the Ship into the air. The Walls were sealed and Eye was guiding them away from the planet.

'We're in open space now,' Talker said. Listening to Pusher, he hoped his mind hadn't cracked. 'Eye and Thinker will give a direction, I'll transmit it to you, and you push along it.'

'You're crazy,' Pusher mumbled. 'You must have the wrong planet. I wish you nightmares would go away.'

'You're in the Co-operation now,' Talker said desperately. 'There's the direction. Push!'

The Pusher didn't do anything for a moment. He was slowly emerging from his fantasy, realizing that he wasn't in a dream, after all. He felt the Co-operation. Eye to Thinker, Thinker to Talker, Talker to Pusher, all inter-co-ordinated with Walls, and with each other.

'What is this?' Pusher asked. He felt the oneness of the Ship, the great warmth, the closeness achieved only in the Co-operation.

He pushed.

Nothing happened.

'Try again,' Talker begged.

Pusher searched his mind. He found a deep well of doubt and fear. Staring into it, he saw his own tortured face.

Thinker illuminated it for him.

Pushers had lived with this doubt and fear for centuries. Pushers had fought through fear, killed through doubt.

That was where the Pusher organ was!

Human – specialist – Pusher – he entered fully into the Crew, merged with them, threw mental arms around the shoulders of Thinker and Talker.

Suddenly, the Ship shot forward at eight times the speed of light. It continued to accelerate.

Seventh Victim

Stanton Frelaine sat at his desk, trying to look as busy as an executive should at nine-thirty in the morning. It was impossible. He couldn't concentrate on the advertisement he had written the previous night, couldn't think about business. All he could do was wait until the mail came.

He had been expecting his notification for two weeks now. The Government was behind schedule, as usual.

The glass door of his office was marked *Morger and Frelaine, Clothiers.* It opened, and E. J. Morger walked in, limping slightly from his old gunshot wound. His shoulders were bent; but at the age of seventy-three, he wasn't worrying much about his posture.

'Well, Stan?' Morger asked. 'What about that ad?'

Frelaine had joined Morger sixteen years ago, when he was twenty-seven. Together they had built Protec-Clothes into a million-dollar concern.

'I suppose you can run it,' Frelaine said, handing the slip of paper to Morger. If only the mail would come earlier, he thought.

'"Do you own a Protec-Suit?"' Morger read aloud, holding the paper close to his eyes. '"The finest tailoring in the world has gone into Morger and Frelaine's Protec-Suit, to make it the leader in men's fashions."'

Morger cleared his throat and glanced at Frelaine. He smiled and read on.

'"Protec-Suit is the safest as well as the smartest. Every Protec-Suit comes with special built-in gun pocket, guaranteed not to bulge. No one will know you are carrying a gun – except you. The gun pocket is exceptionally easy to get at, permitting fast, unhindered draw. Choice of hip or breast pocket." Very nice,' Morger commented.

Frelaine nodded morosely.

'"The Protec-Suit Special has the fling-out gun pocket, the greatest modern advance in personal protection. A touch of the concealed button throws the gun into your hand, cocked, safeties off. Why not drop into the Protec-Store nearest you? *Why not be safe?*"

'That's fine,' Morger said. 'That's a very nice, dignified ad.' He thought for a moment, fingering his white moustache. 'Shouldn't you mention that Protec-Suits come in a variety of styles, single and double-breasted, one and two button rolls, deep and shallow flares?'

'Right. I forgot.'

Frelaine took back the sheet and jotted a note on the edge of it. Then he stood up, smoothing his jacket over his prominent stomach. Frelaine was forty-three, a little overweight, a little bald on top. He was an amiable-looking man with cold eyes.

'Relax.' Morger said. 'It'll come in to-day's mail.'

Frelaine forced himself to smile. He felt like pacing the floor, but instead sat on the edge of the desk.

'You'd think it was my first kill,' he said, with a deprecating smile.

'I know how it is,' Morger said. 'Before I hung up my gun, I couldn't sleep for a month, waiting for a notification. I know.'

The two men waited. Just as the silence was becoming unbearable, the door opened. A clerk walked in and deposited the mail on Frelaine's desk.

Frelaine swung around and gathered up the letters. He thumbed through them rapidly and found what he had been waiting for – the long white envelope from ECB, with the official government seal on it.

'That's it!' Frelaine said, and broke into a grin. 'That's the baby!'

'Fine.' Morger eyed the envelope with interest, but didn't ask Frelaine to open it. It would be a breach of etiquette, as well as a violation in the eyes of the law. No one was supposed to know a Victim's name except his Hunter. 'Have a good hunt.'

'I expect to,' Frelaine replied confidently. His desk was in order – had been for a week. He picked up his briefcase.

'A good kill will do you a world of good,' Morger said, putting his hand lightly on Frelaine's padded shoulder. 'You've been keyed up.'

'I know,' Frelaine grinned again and shook Morger's hand.

'Wish I was a kid again,' Morger said, glancing down at his crippled leg with wryly humorous eyes. 'Makes me want to pick up a gun again.'

The old man had been quite a Hunter in his day. Ten successful hunts had qualified him for the exclusive Tens Club. And, of course, for each hunt Morger had had to act as Victim, so he had twenty kills to his credit.

'I sure hope my Victim isn't anyone like you,' Frelaine said, half in jest.

'Don't worry about it. What number will this be?'

'The seventh.'

'Lucky seven. Go to it,' Morger said. 'We'll get you into the Tens yet.'

Frelaine waved his hand and started out the door.

'Just don't get careless,' warned Morger. 'All it takes is a single slip and I'll need a new partner. If you don't mind, I like the one I've got now.'

'I'll be careful,' Frelaine promised.

Instead of taking a bus, Frelaine walked to his apartment. He wanted time to cool off. There was no sense in acting like a kid on his first kill.

As he walked, Frelaine kept his eyes strictly to the front. Staring at anyone was practically asking for a bullet, if the man happened to be serving as Victim. Some Victims shot if you just glanced at them. Nervous fellows. Frelaine prudently looked above the heads of the people he passed.

Ahead of him was a huge billboard, offering J.F. O'Donovan's services to the public.

'Victims!' the sign proclaimed in huge red letters. 'Why take chances? Use an O'Donovan accredited Spotter. Let us locate your assigned killer. Pay *after* you get him!'

The sign reminded Frelaine. He would call Ed Morrow as soon as he reached his apartment.

He crossed the street, quickening his stride. He could hardly wait to get home now, to open the envelope and discover who his victim was. Would he be clever or stupid? Rich, like Frelaine's fourth Victim, or poor, like the first and second? Would he have an organized Spotter service, or try to go it on his own?

The excitement of the chase was wonderful, coursing through his veins, quickening his heart-beat. From a block or so away, he heard gunfire. Two quick shots, and then a final one.

Somebody got his man, Frelaine thought. Good for him.

It was a superb feeling, he told himself. He was *alive* again.

At his one-room apartment, the first thing Frelaine did was call Ed Morrow, his spotter. The man worked as a garage attendant between calls.

'Hello, Ed? Frelaine.'

'Oh, hi, Mr Frelaine.' He could see the man's thin, grease-stained face, grinning flat-lipped at the telephone.

'I'm going out on one, Ed.'

'Good luck, Mr Frelaine,' Ed Morrow said. 'I suppose you'll want me to stand by?'

'That's right. I don't expect to be gone more than a week or two. I'll probably get my notification of Victim Status within three months of the kill.'

'I'll be standing by. Good hunting, Mr Frelaine.'

'Thanks. So long.' He hung up. It was a wise safety measure to reserve a first-class spotter. After his kill, it would be Frelaine's turn as Victim. Then, once again, Ed Morrow would be his life insurance.

And what a marvellous spotter Morrow was! Uneducated – stupid, really. But what an eye for people! Morrow was a natural. His pale eyes could tell an out-of-towner at a glance. He was diabolically clever at rigging an ambush. An indispensable man.

Frelaine took out the envelope, chuckling to himself remembering some of the tricks Morrow had turned for the Hunters. Still smiling, he glanced at the data inside the envelope.

Janet-Marie Patzig.

His Victim was a female.

Frelaine stood up and paced for a few moments. Then he read the letter again. Janet-Marie Patzig. No mistake. A girl. Three photographs were enclosed, her address, and the usual descriptive data.

Frelaine frowned. He had never killed a female.

He hesitated for a moment, then picked up the telephone and dialled ECB.

'Emotional Catharsis Bureau, Information Section,' a man's voice answered.

'Say, look,' Frelaine said. 'I just got my notification and I pulled a girl. Is that in order?' He gave the clerk the girl's name.

'It's all in order, sir,' the clerk replied after a minute of checking micro-files. 'The girl registered with the board under her own free will. The law says she has the same rights and privileges as a man.'

'Could you tell me how many kills she has?'

'I'm sorry, sir. The only information you're allowed is the Victim's legal status and the descriptive data you have received.'

'I see.' Frelaine paused. 'Could I draw another?'

'You can refuse the hunt, of course. That is your legal right. But you will not be allowed another Victim until you have served. Do you wish to refuse?'

'Oh, no,' Frelaine said hastily. 'I was just wondering. Thank you.'

He hung up and sat down in his largest armchair, loosening his belt. This required some thought.

Damn women, he grumbled to himself, always trying to horn in on a man's game. Why can't they stay home?

But they were free citizens, he reminded himself. Still, it just didn't seem *feminine*.

He knew that, historically speaking, the Emotional Catharsis Board had been established for men and men only. The Board had been formed at the end of the fourth world war – or sixth, as some historians counted it.

At that time there had been a driving need for permanent, lasting peace. The reason was practical, as were the men who engineered it.

Simply – annihilation was just around the corner.

In the world wars, weapons increased in magnitude, efficiency and exterminating power. Soldiers became accustomed to them, less and less reluctant to use them.

But the saturation point had been reached. Another war would truly be the war to end all wars. There would be no one left to start another.

So this peace *had* to last for all time, but the men who engineered it were practical. They recognized the tensions and dislocations still present, the cauldrons in which wars are brewed. They asked themselves why peace had never lasted in the past.

'Because men like to fight,' was their answer.

'Oh, no!' screamed the idealists.

But the men who engineered the peace were forced to

postulate, regretfully, the presence of a need for violence in a large percentage of mankind.

Men aren't angels. They aren't fiends, either. They are just very human beings, with a high degree of combativeness.

With the scientific knowledge and the power they had at that moment, the practical men could have gone a long way towards breeding this trait out of the race. Many thought this was the answer.

The practical men didn't. They recognized the validity of competition, love of battle, courage in the face of overwhelming odds. These, they felt, were admirable traits for a race, and insurance towards its perpetuity. Without them, the race would be bound to retrogress.

The tendency towards violence, they found, was inextricably linked with ingenuity, flexibility, drive.

The problem, then: To arrange a peace that would last after they were gone. To stop the race from destroying itself, without removing the responsible traits.

The way to do this, they decided, was to rechannel Man's violence.

Provide him with an outlet, an expression.

The first big step was the legalization of gladiatorial events, complete with blood and thunder. But more was needed. Sublimations worked only up to a point. Then people demanded the real thing.

There is no substitute for murder.

So murder was legalized, on a strictly individual basis, and only for those who wanted it. The governments were directed to create Emotional Catharsis Boards.

After a period of experimentation, uniform rules were adopted.

Anyone who wanted to murder could sign up at the ECB. Giving certain data and assurances, he would be granted a Victim.

Anyone who signed up to murder, under the government rules, had to take his turn a few months later as Victim – if he survived.

That, in essence, was the set-up. The individual could commit as many murders as he wanted. But between each, he had to be a Victim. If he successfully killed his Hunter, he could stop, or sign up for another murder.

At the end of ten years, an estimated third of the world's civilized population had applied for at least one murder. The number slid to a fourth, and stayed there.

Philosophers shook their heads, but the practical men were satisfied. War was where it belonged – in the hands of the individual.

Of course, there were ramifications to the game, and elaborations. Once its existence had been accepted it became big business. There were services for Victim and Hunter alike.

The Emotional Catharsis Board picked the Victim's names at random. A Hunter was allowed two weeks in which to make his kill. This had to be done by his own ingenuity, unaided. He was given the name of his Victim, address and description, and allowed to use a standard calibre pistol. He could wear no armour of any sort.

The Victim was notified a week before the Hunter. He was told only that he was a Victim. He did not know the name of his Hunter. He was allowed his choice of armour. He could hire spotters. A spotter couldn't kill; only Victim and Hunter could do that. But he could detect a stranger in town, or ferret out a nervous gunman.

The Victim could arrange any kind of ambush in his power to kill the Hunter.

There were stiff penalties for killing or wounding the wrong man, for no other murder was allowed. Grudge killings or gain killings were punishable by death.

The beauty of the system was that the people who wanted to kill could do so. Those who didn't – the bulk of the population – didn't have to.

At least, there weren't any more big wars. Not even the imminence of one.

Just hundreds of thousands of small ones.

Frelaine didn't especially like the idea of killing a woman; but she *had* signed up. It wasn't his fault. And he wasn't going to lose out on his seventh hunt.

He spent the rest of the morning memorizing the data on his Victim, then filed the letter.

Janet Patzig lived in New York. That was good. He enjoyed hunting in a big city, and he had always wanted to see New York. Her age wasn't given, but to judge from her photographs, she was in her early twenties.

Frelaine phoned for his jet reservations to New York, then took a shower. He dressed with care in a new Protec-Suit Special made for the occasion. From his collection he selected a gun, cleaned and oiled it, and fitted it into the fling-out pocket of the suit. Then he packed his suitcase.

A pulse of excitement was pounding in his veins. Strange, he thought, how each killing was a new thrill. It was something you just didn't tire of, the way you did of

French pastry or women or drinking or anything else. It was always new and different.

Finally, he looked over his books to see which he would take.

His library contained all the good books on the subject. He wouldn't need any of his Victim books, like L. Fred Tracy's *Tactics for the Victim*, with its insistence on a rigidly controlled environment, or Dr Frisch's *Don't Think Like a Victim!*

He would be very interested in those in a few months, when he was a Victim again. Now he wanted hunting books.

Tactics for Hunting Humans was the standard and definitive work, but he had it almost memorized. *Development of the Ambush* was not adapted to his present needs.

He chose *Hunting in Cities*, by Mitwell and Clark, *Spotting the Spotter*, by Algreen, and *The Victim's In-group*, by the same author.

Everything was in order. He left a note for the milkman, locked his apartment and took a cab to the airport.

In New York, he checked into a hotel in the mid-town area, not too far from his Victim's address. The clerks were smiling and attentive, which bothered Frelaine. He didn't like to be recognized so easily as an out-of-town killer.

The first thing he saw in his room was a pamphlet on his bed-table. *How to Get the Most out of your Emotional Catharsis*, it was called, with the compliments of the management. Frelaine smiled and thumbed through it

Since it was his first visit to New York, he spent the afternoon just walking the streets in his Victim's neighbourhood. After that, he wandered through a few stores.

Martinson and Black was a fascinating place. He went through their Hunter–Hunted room. There were lightweight bullet-proof vests for Victims, and Richard Arlington hats, with bullet-proof crowns.

On one side was a large display of a new .38 calibre sidearm.

'Use the Malvern Straight-shot!' the ad proclaimed. 'ECB-approved. Carries a load of twelve shots. Tested deviation less than .001 inches for 1,000 feet. Don't miss your Victim! Don't risk your life without the best! Be safe with Malvern!

Frelaine smiled. The ad. was good, and the small black weapon looked ultimately efficient. But he was satisfied with the one he had.

There was a special sale on trick canes, with concealed four-shot magazine, promising safety and concealment. As a young man, Frelaine had gone in heavily for novelties. But now he knew that the old-fashioned ways were usually best.

Outside the store, four men from the Department of Sanitation were carting away a freshly killed corpse. Frelaine regretted missing the take.

He ate dinner in a good restaurant and went to bed early.

Tomorrow he had a lot to do.

The next day, with the face of his Victim before him, Frelaine walked through her neighbourhood. He didn't look closely at anyone. Instead, he moved rapidly, as though he were really going somewhere, the way an old Hunter should walk.

He passed several bars and dropped into one for a

drink. Then he went on, down a side street off Lexington Avenue.

There was a pleasant pavement café there. Frelaine walked past it.

And there she was! He could never mistake the face. It was Janet Patzig, seated at a table, staring into a drink. She didn't look up as he passed.

Frelaine walked to the end of the block. He turned the corner and stopped, hands trembling.

Was the girl crazy, exposing herself in the open? Did she think she had a charmed life?

He hailed a taxi and had the man drive around the block. Sure enough, she was just sitting there. Frelaine took a careful look.

She seemed younger than her pictures, but he couldn't be sure. He would guess her to be not much over twenty. Her dark hair was parted in the middle and combed above her ears, giving her a nun-like appearance. Her expression, as far as Frelaine could tell, was one of resigned sadness.

Wasn't she even going to make an attempt to defend herself?

Frelaine paid the driver and hurried to a drugstore. Finding a vacant telephone booth, he called ECB.

'Are you sure that a Victim named Janet-Marie Patzig has been notified?'

'Hold on, sir.' Frelaine tapped on the door while the clerk looked up the information. 'Yes, sir. We have her personal confirmation. Is there anything wrong, sir?'

'No,' Frelaine said. 'Just wanted to check.'

After all, it was no one's business if the girl didn't want to defend herself.

He was still entitled to kill her.

It was his turn.

He postponed it for that day, however, and went to a cinema. After dinner, he returned to his room and read the ECB pamphlet. Then he lay on his bed and glared at the ceiling.

All he had to do was pump a bullet into her. Just ride by in a cab and kill her.

She was being a very bad sport about it, he decided resentfully, and went to sleep.

The next afternoon, Frelaine walked by the café again. The girl was back, sitting at the same table. Frelaine caught a cab.

'Drive around the block very slowly,' he told the driver.

'Sure,' the driver said, grinning with sardonic wisdom.

From the cab, Frelaine watched for spotters. As far as he could tell, the girl had none. Both her hands were in sight upon the table.

An easy, stationary target.

Frelaine touched the button of his double-breasted jacket. A fold flew open and the gun was in his hand. He broke it open and checked the cartridges, then closed it with a snap.

'Slowly, now,' he told the driver.

The taxi crawled by the café. Frelaine took careful aim, centring the girl in his sights. His finger tightened on the trigger.

'Damn it!' he said.

A waiter had passed by the girl. He didn't want to chance winging someone else.

'Around the block again,' he told the driver.

The man gave him another grin and hunched down in his seat. Frelaine wondered if the driver would feel so happy if he knew that Frelaine was gunning for a woman.

This time there was no waiter around. The girl was lighting a cigarette, her mournful face intent on her lighter. Frelaine centred her in his sights, squarely above the eyes, and held his breath.

Then he shook his head and put the gun back in his pocket.

The idiotic girl was robbing him of the full benefit of his catharsis.

He paid the driver and started to walk.

It's too easy, he told himself. He was used to a real chase. Most of the other six kills had been quite difficult. The Victims had tried every dodge. One had hired at least a dozen spotters. But Frelaine had reached them all by altering his tactics to meet the situation.

Once he had dressed as a milkman, another time as a bill collector. The sixth Victim he had had to chase through the Sierra Nevadas. The man had clipped him, too. But Frelaine had done better.

How could he be proud of this one? What would the Tens Club say?

That brought Frelaine up with a start. He wanted to get into the club. Even if he passed up this girl he would have to defend himself against a Hunter. If he survived, he would still be four hunts away from membership. At that rate, he might never get in.

He began to pass the café again, then, on impulse, stopped abruptly.

'Hello,' he said.

Janet Patzig looked at him out of sad blue eyes, but said nothing.

'Say, look,' he said, sitting down. 'If I'm being fresh, just tell me and I'll go. I'm an out-of-towner. Here on a convention. And I'd just like someone feminine to talk to. If you'd rather I didn't—'

'I don't care,' Janet Patzig said tonelessly.

'A brandy,' Frelaine told the waiter. Janet Patzig's glass was still half full.

Frelaine looked at the girl and he could feel his heart throbbing against his ribs. This was more like it – having a drink with your Victim!

'My name's Stanton Frelaine,' he said, knowing it didn't matter.

'Janet.'

'Janet what?'

'Janet Patzig.'

'Nice to know you,' Frelaine said, in a perfectly natural voice. 'Are you doing anything tonight Janet?'

'I'm probably being killed tonight,' she said quietly.

Frelaine looked at her carefully. Did she realize who he was? For all he knew, she had a gun levelled at him under the table.

He kept his hand close to the fling-out button.

'Are you a Victim?' he asked.

'You guessed it,' she said sardonically. 'If I were you, I'd stay out of the way. No sense getting hit by mistake.'

Frelaine couldn't understand the girl's calm. Was she a suicide? Perhaps she just didn't care. Perhaps she wanted to die.

'Haven't you got any spotters?' he asked, with the right expression of amazement.

'No.' She looked at him, full in the face, and Frelaine saw something he hadn't noticed before.

She was very lovely.

'I am a bad, bad girl,' she said lightly. 'I got the idea I'd like to commit a murder, so I signed for ECB. Then – I couldn't do it.'

Frelaine shook his head, sympathizing with her.

'But I'm still in, of course. Even if I didn't shoot, I still have to be a Victim.'

'But why don't you hire some spotters?' he asked.

'I couldn't kill anyone,' she said. 'I just couldn't. I don't even have a gun.'

'You've got a lot of courage,' Frelaine said, 'coming out in the open this way.' Secretly, he was amazed at her stupidity.

'What can I do?' she asked listlessly. 'You can't hide from a Hunter. Not a real one. And I don't have enough money to make a good disappearance.'

'Since it's in your own defence, I should think—' Frelaine began, but she interrupted.

'No. I've made up my mind on that. This whole thing is wrong, the whole system. When I had my Victim in the sights – when I saw how easily I could – I could—'

She pulled herself together quickly.

'Oh, let's forget it,' she said and smiled.

Frelaine found her smile dazzling.

After that, they talked of other things. Frelaine told her of his business, and she told him about New York. She was twenty-two, an unsuccessful actress.

They had supper together. When she accepted Frelaine's invitation to go to the Gladiatorials, he felt absurdly elated.

He called a cab – he seemed to be spending his entire time in New York in cabs – and opened the door for her. She started in. Frelaine hesitated. He could have pumped a shot into her at that moment. It would have been very easy.

But he held back. Just for the moment, he told himself.

The Gladiatorials were about the same as those held anywhere else, except that the talent was a little better. There were the usual historical events, swordsmen and netmen, duels with sabre and foil.

Most of these, naturally, were fought to the death.

Then bull-fighting, lion-fighting and rhino-fighting, followed by the more modern events. Fights from behind barricades with bow and arrow. Duelling on a high wire.

The evening passed pleasantly.

Frelaine escorted the girl home, the palms of his hands sticky with sweat. He had never found a woman he liked better. And yet she was his legitimate kill.

He didn't know what he was going to do.

She invited him in and they sat together on the couch. The girl lighted a cigarette for herself with a large lighter, then settled back.

'Are you leaving soon?' she asked him.

'I suppose so,' Frelaine said. 'The convention is only lasting another day.'

She was silent for a moment. 'I'll be sorry to see you go.'

They were quiet for a while. Then Janet went to fix him a drink. Frelaine eyed her retreating back. Now was the time. He placed his hand near the button.

But the moment had passed for him, irrevocably. He wasn't going to kill her. You don't kill the girl you love.

The realization that he loved her was shocking. He'd come to kill, not to find a wife.

She came back with the drink and sat down opposite him, staring at emptiness.

'Janet,' he said. 'I love you.'

She sat, just looking at him. There were tears in her eyes.

'You can't,' she protested. 'I'm a Victim. I won't live long enough to—'

'You won't be killed. I'm your Hunter.'

She stared at him a moment, then laughed uncertainly. 'Are you going to kill me?' she asked.

'Don't be ridiculous,' he said. 'I'm going to marry you.'

Suddenly she was in his arms.

'Oh, Lord!' she gasped. 'The waiting – I've been so frightened—'

'It's all over,' he told her. 'Think what a story it'll make for our kids. How I came to murder you and left marrying you.'

She kissed him, then sat back and lighted another cigarette.

'Let's start packing,' Frelaine said. 'I want—'

'Wait,' Janet interrupted. 'You haven't asked if *I* love *you*.'

'What?'

She was still smiling, and the cigarette lighter was

pointed at him. In the bottom of it was a black hole. A hole just large enough for a .38 calibre bullet.

'Don't kid around,' he objected, getting to his feet.

'I'm not being funny, darling,' she said.

In a fraction of a second, Frelaine had time to wonder how he could ever have thought she was not much over twenty. Looking at her now – *really* looking at her – he knew she couldn't be much less than thirty. Every minute of her strained, tense existence showed on her face.

'I don't love you, Stanton,' she said very softly, the cigarette lighter poised.

Frelaine struggled for breath. One part of him was able to realize detachedly what a marvellous actress she really was. She must have known all along.

Frelaine pushed the button, and the gun was in his hand, cocked and ready.

The blow that struck him in the chest knocked him over a coffee table. The gun fell out of his hand. Gasping, half-conscious, he watched her take careful aim for the *coup de grâce*.

'Now I can join the Tens,' he heard her say elatedly as she squeezed the trigger.

Dimension of Miracles

ROBERT SHECKLEY

'Hilarious SF satire. Douglas Adams said it was the only thing like *The Hitchhiker's Guide to the Galaxy*, written ten years earlier. It's wonderful'
  Neil Gaiman

This madcap cosmic farce relates the adventures of the hapless human Carmody, as he attempts to make his way home to Earth after winning the grand prize in the Intergalactic Sweepstake, encountering parallel worlds, incompetent bureaucrats and talking dinosaurs on the way.

'The greatest entertainer ever produced by science fiction … a feast of wit and intelligence'
  J. G. Ballard

ISBN 9780241472491

Ten Thousand Light-Years From Home

JAMES TIPTREE JR.

'Unquestionably one of the brightest-burning talents in
the constellation of science fiction'
The New York Times

Written under a pseudonym, the pioneering and outlandish tales of Alice B. Sheldon are some of the greatest science
fiction short stories of the twentieth century, telling of dys-
topian chases, alien sex and the loneliness of the universe.

'What her work brought to the genre was a blend of lyri-
cism and inventiveness, as if some poet had rewritten a
number of clever SF standards and then passed them on
to a psychoanalyst'
Brian Aldiss

ISBN 9780241469231

Driftglass

SAMUEL R. DELANY

'Delany's works have become essential to the history of science fiction.'

New Yorker

Samuel R. Delany is one of the most radical and influential science fiction writers of our age, who reinvented the genre with his fearless explorations of race, class and gender. *Driftglass* is the definitive volume of his stories, featuring neutered space travellers, telepathy, Hells Angels and genetically modified amphibious workers.

'Delany's books interweave science fiction with histories of race, sexuality and control. In so doing, he gives readers fiction that reflects and explores the social truths of our world.'

The New York Times

ISBN 9780241510575

Robot

ADAM WIŚNIEWSKI-SNERG

'We have given you life . . . so that you could discover a fraction of the great secret.'

Is BER-66 a human or a robot? His controllers, known as 'the Mechanism,' tell him he is a living machine, programmed to gather information on the inhabitants of the strange underground world he finds himself in. But as he penetrates its tunnels and locked rooms, encountering mysterious doppelgangers and a petrified city, he comes closer to the truth of his existence. Considered one of the most important Polish science fiction novels of all time, *Robot* is a haunting philosophical enquiry into the nature of our reality and our place in the universe.

'An instant classic which catapulted Snerg to the rank of Poland's best sf authors.'
  Science Fiction Encyclopedia

ISBN 9780241485118

The Hair-Carpet Weavers

ANDREAS ESCHBACH

Translated by Doryl Jensen

In a distant universe, since the beginning of time, workers have spent their lives weaving intricate carpets from the hair of women and girls. But why? Andreas Eschbach's mysterious, poignant space opera explores the absurdity of work and of life itself.

'A novel of ideas that evokes complex emotions through the working out of an intricate and ultimately satisfying plot'

The New York Times Book Review

ISBN 9780241454718

Trafalgar

ANGÉLICA GORODISCHER

Translated by Amalia Gladhart

Part pulp adventure, part otherworldly meditation, this is the story of Trafalgar Medrano: intergalactic trader and lover of bitter coffee and black cigarettes. In the bars and cafés of Rosario, Argentina, he recounts tall tales of his space escapades – involving, among other things, time travel and dancing troglodytes.

'A kind of magical realism for science fiction … Quite, quite brilliant'
  Tor

'A unique brand of science fiction … unlike anything I've ever read'
  Los Angeles Review of Books

ISBN 9780241467961

The Cyberiad

STANISLAW LEM

Translated by Michael Kandel

'A giant of twentieth-century science fiction'
  Guardian

One of the world's most beloved science-fiction writers, Stanislaw Lem was famed for his wryly comic, outlandish imaginings of the relationship between humans and technology. In this playful cosmic fantasia, two 'constructors' compete to dream up ever more ingenious inventions in a universe beyond reality.

'A Jorge Luis Borges for the Space Age, who plays with every concept of philosophy and physics'
  The New York Times

ISBN 9780241467992

One Billion Years to the End of the World

ARKADY AND BORIS STRUGATSKY

Translated by Antonina W. Bouis

This mordantly funny and provocative tale from Soviet Russia's leading science-fiction writers is the story of astrophysicist Dmitri Malianov. As he reaches a major breakthrough, he finds himself plagued by interruptions, from a mysterious crate of vodka to a glamorous woman on his doorstep. Is the Universe trying to tell him something?

'A beautiful book'
  Ursula K. Le Guin

'On putting down one of their books, you feel a cold breeze still lifting the hairs on the back of your neck'
  The New York Times

ISBN 9780241472477